W9-BPK-607

GINNIE AND GENEVA

Ginnie and her mother and the principal of Lincoln School all sat in the principal's office. Somewhere in this school, Ginnie thought, there are girls who will be my friends. What are their names? What are they doing right now?

As soon as Ginnie enters room 4B, her excitement about starting school for the first time fades. When the teacher introduces her to the class, Ginnie can feel the blush creeping into her cheeks as everyone looks up to stare at the new girl. With trembling legs, Ginnie takes a seat at her desk and sits there quietly, not looking at anyone. *Will I make any friends here?* Ginnie wonders. She hopes all her wonderful dreams of school aren't going to turn into one big nightmare.

Also by Catherine Wooley

CATHY LEONARD CALLING

GINNIE & GENEVA

BY CATHERINE WOOLLEY

PUFFIN BOOKS

PUFFIN BOOKS

Published by the Penguin Group

Viking Penguin Inc., 40 West 23rd Street, New York, New York 10010, U.S.A.

Penguin Books Ltd, 27 Wrights Lane, London W8 5TZ England

Penguin Books Australia Ltd, Ringwood, Victoria, Australia

Penguin Books Canada Ltd, 2801 John Street, Markham, Ontario, Canada L3R 1B4

Penguin Books (N.Z.) Ltd, 182–190 Wairau Road, Auckland 10, New Zealand

Penguin Books Ltd, Registered Offices: Harmondsworth, Middlesex, England

First published in the United States of America by William Morrow & Company, Inc., 1961
Published in Puffin Books, 1988 by arrangement with William Morrow & Company, Inc.

Copyright © Catherine Woolley 1948
All rights reserved

Printed in the United States of America by R. R. Donnelley & Sons Company,
Harrisonburg, Virginia
Set in Garamond #3

Library of Congress Cataloging in Publication Data
Woolley, Catherine.   Ginnie and Geneva.
Summary: When Ginnie's family settles in a new home,
she gets to go to a real school for the first time,
only it isn't so much fun as she'd hoped.
[1. Schools—Fiction]   2. Moving, Household—
Fiction]   I. Title.
PZ7.W882Gi   1988   [Fic]   87-36045   ISBN 0-14-032550-6

Except in the United States of America, this book is sold subject to the
condition that it shall not, by the way of trade or otherwise, be lent, re-
sold, hired out, or otherwise circulated without the publisher's prior
consent in any form of binding or cover other than that in which it is
published and without a similar condition including this condition being
imposed on the subsequent purchaser.

CONTENTS

GINNIE AND GENEVA

THE FIRST DAY

Ginnie and her mother and the principal of Lincoln School all sat in the principal's office.

Ginnie sat up straight, her toes on the floor, holding the chair with both hands. Her heart beat fast with excitement.

She was conscious of a pleasant warmth on her back from the September morning sunshine pouring in the windows. A million specks of dust floated in the sunlight as it streamed across Miss Yates' desk.

There was a clean brown blotter on the desk, and a green plant and a row of books. The air coming in the open window gently stirred the corner of a paper in the pile under the marble paperweight. From outside, somewhere in the quiet morning, drifted the tinkle of bells from a junkman's wagon.

All these things Ginnie noticed with the edges of her mind. Her eyes were on Miss Yates. It was Miss Yates who was going to let her come to Lincoln School!

Miss Yates' eyes twinkled at Ginnie pleasantly behind her glasses. The principal saw a rather thin, long-legged little girl, in a rose-colored gingham dress, with rose-colored bows on her short, light brown braids. She saw wide hazel eyes looking at her expectantly.

"I'm glad you're here for the first day of school, Georgina," she said kindly.

Ginnie's face lighted up. "So'm I glad!" she said in a soft little voice, beaming at Miss Yates.

The principal thought quickly, This child is not so plain when she smiles.

Miss Yates turned to Ginnie's mother. "You say Georgina has never been to school before?"

"No," Mother replied. "Her father has

4

traveled on business. Ginnie and I have always gone with him. I used to be a teacher," Mother explained. "I've taught her. But now we're settled here. I'm sure she's ready to go into the fourth grade."

Miss Yates had it all clear now. She nodded. She turned in her swivel chair, picked up her pen, and wrote on the orange card on her desk.

"Name, Georgina Fellows," Miss Yates murmured. "Age, nine."

Ginnie sighed. She was tired, sitting up straight. She wriggled back and rested her head.

But her head kept popping up. It was so hard to sit still! Excitement was hopping and skipping inside her.

"What is your address, Georgina?" The scratching of the pen stopped.

Instantly Ginnie's head came up and she slid forward again. "Eighty-two R-red Robin Lane," she said breathlessly.

She watched the principal's firm-looking hand move capably across the card. Somewhere in this school, Ginnie was thinking as her eyes followed the pen, there are girls who will be my friends. What are their names? What are they doing this minute?

It seemed strange, and mysterious some-how. She had no idea who they were, and they didn't know about her. Yet in a little while they would find each other!

Ginnie drew a quick breath and moved impatiently.

Miss Yates blotted the ink and pushed back her chair. "We'll see how things go," she said. "I'll take you up to 4-B now."

Ginnie and Mother stood up too. A great thrill of excitement rushed up Ginnie's spine. Then, just as quickly, a shy little fear ran down it. It almost made the eagerness go away.

"You're going into a lovely class," Miss Yates said. She smiled at Ginnie again. "You're glad to be going to school, aren't you?"

"Oh, yes!" Ginnie gasped, even though her knees were all trembly at the prospect.

"Good-by." Mother leaned down. Ginnie stood on tiptoe to throw her arms around her neck. She felt a sudden lonesomeness at leaving Mother.

But Miss Yates was waiting. Holding the principal's hand, Ginnie went down the corridor. They turned the corner. Now Mother was left behind.

Ginnie was really in school at last!

The 4-B room was large and light. Ginnie was conscious of windows, with sun pouring in, along one side and the back. There was a blackboard across the front. The room had a strong smell of fresh paint and the sweet sourness of apples.

The room was filled with children. Ginnie saw that in one startled glance. She was suddenly so overcome with shyness she couldn't raise her eyes. The teacher glanced up.

"Miss Roberts, this is Georgina Fellows, a new pupil." Miss Yates handed her Ginnie's card.

"We're happy to have you, Georgina," Miss Roberts said. "Now, let me see. Suppose you take the fifth desk here in the fourth row."

Ginnie found her way to the desk, tiptoeing to be less conspicuous. Her legs trembled. The blood pounded in her ears. As she slipped into her seat, eyes seemed to be boring holes in her back.

She fixed her gaze firmly on Miss Roberts. Why, she hadn't known she'd be so scared! She didn't dare turn her head the tiniest bit.

On Miss Roberts' desk were piles of books. The teacher got a red-headed boy and a dark, curly-haired boy to pass them out.

The first was a geography. It was new and sent up a fresh paper-and-ink smell. Ginnie opened the book, flattening the pages at front and back with the palm of her hand. A picture of a mountain, a camel, a strange building caught her eye.

Ginnie settled into her seat. She felt safer, more at home, with the book in the circle of her arm.

Miss Roberts was holding a pile of yellow paper.

"While I'm checking the numbers of the books," she said, "you may write a composition. What would you like to write about?"

A plump, pink-cheeked girl in the next

row waved her hand. Miss Roberts nodded at her, smiling. "Tell me your name first," she said.

"Elaine Elizabeth Porter," the plump girl said instantly.

Ginnie was surprised to hear a sort of gasp run plainly through the room. Miss Roberts looked surprised too. "That will do!" she said. "Now, Elaine?"

A snicker. Louder this time. The color rose in Miss Roberts' checks.

Elaine looked, innocent and round-eyed, at the teacher. "I'd like to write about what we did this summer."

"That's a good idea, Elaine!"

This time the class practically laughed out loud. Miss Roberts could ignore it no longer. "What is so funny?" she exclaimed.

"They're just silly," Elaine replied.

"Well, stop being silly." The teacher looked stern. "And write your compositions." She passed the paper to the monitors.

Ginnie took up her pencil, wondering what the laughing had been about. She felt sorry for Miss Roberts. She glanced over at Elaine

9

with interest. Elaine hadn't minded the laughing at all!

Ginnie settled down happily to write her composition. "This summer we moved into our new house. Our house is white. It has a front yard and a back yard," she wrote.

Then her thoughts began to wander again. Miss Roberts moved up the aisle, writing the numbers of the books on her chart. Ginnie's eyes followed her. Miss Roberts looked nice. Her hair was red-gold, in a smooth roll. She wore a golden-brown dress, the color of autumn leaves.

Ginnie glanced over at Elaine. Why, what was she laughing at?

Elaine was giggling behind her hand. She caught Ginnie's eyes and pointed to a little girl ahead of them. The girl was writing slowly, forming each word with her mouth. Ginnie smiled.

Elaine grabbed her pencil and began to write, making a face with every word.

Ginnie turned back to her composition, a little worried. Elaine shouldn't be mean like that!

"I have never lived in a house before," Ginnie wrote. "But I have lived in lots of hotels."

She finished and put the pencil down.

Suddenly Ginnie sat up and stared. That boy opposite Elaine. Blond, serious, with glasses. He was the one who lived next door!

Peter Ladd his name was. Peter had been away with his family. He had only got home the day before. She had seen him in the yard. She had wanted to say hello but hadn't dared.

Ginnie's thoughts hopped around like persistent mosquitoes. Peter looked like a nice boy. Now that they were in the same class, would she get to know him? Would he play with her?

She had never had a real friend. Once she had found a little girl she liked in a hotel. But before they had a chance to play, Daddy and Mother and Ginnie had had to move. She remembered how she had cried at leaving the little girl.

It was hard to believe that now she would really have friends! Ginnie gave a little sigh of happiness.

11

The recess bell put an end to the writing. The monitors collected the papers and Miss Roberts dismissed the class.

Shyness crept back over Ginnie as she filed out with the other girls. They were all chattering and giggling together. No one paid any attention to her. Ginnie began to feel lonely and a little homesick. When they reached the playground the girls broke into a run. Ginnie followed slowly.

They were starting a tag game. She had never played tag, but she had watched sometimes. She looked on now. Suddenly someone beckoned to her.

"Come on and play!" Elaine shouted.

Ginnie stepped forward eagerly. They wanted her to play!

"Tag! You're it!" Elaine slapped her on the arm and ran.

Ginnie stood still, uncertain what to do. "Do . . . do I chase you?" she asked.

Elaine put her hands on her hips. "Hey, didn't you ever play tag before?" she demanded.

The girls all looked at Ginnie and laughed

12

as if that was the funniest thing they had ever heard of.

Ginnie hesitated. The color rose in her cheeks and her heart beat uncomfortably.

"Come on," Elaine said, "if you're going to play. Chase anyone, dopey!"

Ginnie forced her legs forward. I won't tell them, she thought, that I really never did play before. They'd think I was funny.

Elaine danced before her like a naughty pixie. Finally Ginnie paused to get her breath.

"Can't catch me, can't catch me," Elaine chanted.

Ginnie ran this way, that way. Girl after girl slipped, laughing, from her reach.

She couldn't catch anyone! She blinked hard to keep from crying. Then she made a desperate lunge at Elaine, almost stumbling. Elaine ducked and headed across the playground.

Dong! The hollow gong rang, calling them in to school.

Elaine stopped. "Game's over. And you're still *it!*" She pointed her finger at Ginnie. Then she turned to walk beside her, suddenly pleasant. "What's your name, anyway?"

13

"Georgina Fellows."

"Oh. Mine's really Geneva Porter."

Ginnie opened her eyes and looked at Geneva in amazement.

"I just told Miss Roberts it was Elaine for a joke. She's new this year. That's why all the kids laughed."

"Oh!" Ginnie gasped. "How did you dare?"

"Pooh!" Geneva kicked the gravel as she strode along. "Who's afraid of the old teacher!"

By the time they were back in the 4-B room Miss Roberts had learned the joke too.

"Who can tell me," she asked, "how far you got in history last term?"

Geneva's hand waved.

"Well," Miss Roberts said, "Elaine Elizabeth Geneva Porter?"

Geneva's mouth was open for the answer. She shut it in surprise. There was a roar of laughter. This time Ginnie laughed too.

"You didn't think you'd fool me long, did you?" Miss Roberts asked pleasantly.

"Well, Elizabeth's my middle name anyway," Geneva said. "Couldn't you call me that? Because I don't like Geneva."

"You can be Elizabeth outside of school," Miss Roberts replied, "or Jessie or Josephine or whatever you want. But I'm afraid you'll have to be Geneva here."

Being found out didn't disturb Geneva a bit. While Miss Roberts was writing on the board, she leaned over and offered Ginnie a stick of gum. Ginnie hesitated. Miss Roberts might not like her to chew it. But she took the gum. Geneva popped hers in her mouth.

Once Geneva laughed right out loud when nobody else did. Ginnie stole a look at her. Geneva wasn't afraid of anything! Ginnie looked at the pink, plump cheeks and the short, glossy dark bob.

She didn't like Geneva. She had decided that during recess. But somehow, even if Geneva was mean, she couldn't help admiring her. Geneva seemed so sure of herself.

Geneva was mean, all right. When Peter put on his glasses, Geneva went through the motions of putting on glasses too. Peter's ears turned bright red. But he prenteded not to notice.

At noon Ginnie walked home alone.

Somehow school wasn't the way she had thought it would be. She didn't feel excited any more.

She learned several names that afternoon. The pretty girl on her other side was Marjorie. There were twins in the class—Lucy and Leonard. That small girl with the shy smile and the shabby clothes—the one Geneva had made fun of when she wrote—was named Anna.

Three-twenty came. It seemed years to Ginnie since nine that morning. Her heart grew lighter as she piled her books and waited for the bell.

She was out of the building at last. Someone called her name. Geneva caught up. "Which way do you go?" Geneva asked.

"That way," Ginnie said.

"Oh, I go the other. Well, g'by. See you tomorrow." Geneva raced off, calling to a group of girls.

Ginnie walked along thoughtfully. What a strange girl! First she was mean. Then she was nice. Ginnie was glad Geneva lived in

16

the other direction. She was afraid of Geneva.

But as she turned into Red Robin Lane and saw the white house, Ginnie's spirits suddenly soared. There was Mother, watching for her.

She would change out of her school clothes and get some bread and butter and grape jelly. She would sling her darling black kitty, Mumbo, over one shoulder.

Then she would curl up on the davenport with her book, and forget all about school and girls who were unkind.

GINNIE WALKS ON TIPTOE

It was the second day of school. Ginnie stood at the blackboard, working an arithmetic example. On paper it would have been easy. But subtracting in front of the class flustered her and she had to erase twice.

Beside her, Geneva worked her example. Miss Roberts had stepped into the hall to speak to another teacher.

"S-s!" Geneva whispered sidewise.

Ginnie kept her eyes on her work. Her face flushed as she remembered the tag game yesterday, and how Geneva and the others had laughed at her.

18

She finished her example hurriedly. Then she put down her chalk and tiptoed to her seat.

She had just reached her desk when a low but unmistakable snicker swept the room. Startled, Ginnie jerked up her head. But they weren't looking at her. They were looking behind her.

She turned. Geneva, who always tramped flat on her feet, was returning to her seat on high, exaggerated tiptoes.

Ginnie's heart jumped. Geneva was copying the way she walked! She tried to smile, as if she found it funny too, but the corners of her mouth trembled. She slid into her seat, hiding her face.

Miss Roberts came in and they went on with the arithmetic lesson. Ginnie felt too awful to know what she was doing. How could she ever face the class again!

Suddenly her face grew hot as she thought how silly she must look, always walking on her toes. She hadn't realized she was doing it. She picked up her pencil and stared at the figures on her paper. Oh, Geneva was mean!

Then Ginnie set her jaw firmly. Well, what

19

did she care if a fresh tomboy did make fun of her! She knew more than Geneva knew, anyway. She'd read more books than Geneva—she was sure of that. Ginnie raised her head defiantly.

All morning Geneva ignored her. It was as if she had shot her arrow at Ginnie and was no longer interested. Ginnie kept a wary eye on Geneva, though she pretended to be so interested in her work she didn't look at anyone.

That was how she happened to see Geneva reach over and turn Peter's seat up while he was at the teacher's desk. Ginnie gave a gasp. Would Peter see it?

Peter came back to his seat, not looking. He sat down. Bang! He slid clear through to the floor under his desk.

The class howled with laughter, Geneva harder than anyone. Even Ginnie couldn't keep her face straight. Peter got up, his face scarlet.

"Why, Peter!" Miss Roberts was trying to keep from laughing herself. "What happened to you?"

Peter muttered to himself as he turned his

seat down and sat in it. He didn't look in Geneva's direction. But, Ginnie thought, he must know who did it.

At recess Ginnie ate the apple she brought, standing near the school door. Then she took a walk by herself, keeping carefully away from the tag game. She wondered if the bell was late in ringing, recess seemed so long.

Again at noon she walked home alone. She was quiet at lunch. Mother looked at her thoughtfully once or twice. Ginnie didn't want to tell Mother about the tiptoeing. She felt too awful when she thought of it.

It was during afternoon recess that the thing happened. Ginnie was walking slowly by herself when suddenly, with a rush and a scuffling of feet, the girls were around her. Ginnie turned, startled.

Geneva was spokesman. "Hey," Geneva said, "somebody said you've never been to school before. Haven't you?"

Ginnie tried to back away.

"Haven't you?" Geneva repeated.

Ginnie shook her head desperately, looking around for some way to escape.

21

They stared at her. As if I was a . . . an ant-eater or something in the zoo, Ginnie thought.

"Then how come you're in our class?" Geneva demanded.

"B-because my mother taught me the other grades."

"Oh." Geneva stared at her again. "Then I guess that's why you act so funny, and don't know how to play tag."

Suddenly, facing that circle of faces, Ginnie felt a wave of dislike. Dislike of school, of girls who knew each other and played tag and thought she was queer.

If she could just go home! If she could run down that street, shadowed and peaceful under its arching trees, away from the sounds of school.

The playground was hot in the full glare of the sun, noisy and crowded with shouting, running children, having fun, not caring about her. And she had to stay here.

"Hey, kids, come on! Let's play," Geneva cried. They raced off, leaving her behind, as if she wasn't worth another thought.

The tears sprang to Ginnie's eyes. She

looked quickly around to be sure no one was watching.

She no longer admired or envied Geneva. She hated her! She hated all of them. And this was school, that she had been looking forward to so eagerly.

"That's why you act so funny, and don't know how to play tag," Geneva had said.

Well, she'd keep away. She'd never play tag again, or any other game. They wouldn't have another chance to laugh at her.

Maybe Mother would let her stay home. If she only would!

After school she changed her dress, then come downstairs. Mother was making a new skirt for her, of soft blue and white wool.

"Mother," she said in a low voice, "I wish I didn't have to go to school."

Mother put down her work. "Why, Ginnie?"

Ginnie looked at the floor. "I just don't like it very much."

"But you were so anxious to go!"

Ginnie said nothing.

"Has anything happened?"

23

Oh, Ginnie thought, I'm not going to tell! Even Mother.

Mother said, "I'm sure you'll like school when you get used to it and make friends."

Friends! She wanted no friends. "I'd rather stay here with you," Ginnie said.

"You're not having trouble with the work?"

"Oh, no!"

"Then tell me what's wrong. Maybe we can straighten it out with Miss Roberts."

"No!" Ginnie didn't want Miss Roberts to know. She might say something before the class. I'd just die! Ginnie thought.

"But you can't stay home, Ginnie," Mother said. "If you can't tell me what's wrong you must try and work it out for yourself."

Mother put the needle in her work. "Come here, darling," she said. She put her hand under Ginnie's chin. Ginnie's tears suddenly brimmed over.

"There now," Mother said, holding her close. "Everything's coming out all right!"

The rest of that week Ginnie kept as far away from the other girls as she could. In school she paid strict attention to her work and to Miss Roberts. She never looked at Geneva. Geneva never looked at her.

At recess, Ginnie stayed as far as she could from the tag game.

Friday morning, walking slowly about the playground, she turned a corner and came suddenly on Anna, the small girl with the shabby clothes. Anna was sitting on the little ledge made by a basement window. She was eating a cracker and watching the tag game at a distance.

Anna looked up, startled, as Ginnie came around the corner. Then she smiled.

"Hello," Anna said.

Anna hadn't been in the tag game, Ginnie remembered now, or with the group who had surrounded her to ask questions.

"Want to sit down?" Anna moved over. There was a shy eagerness in her voice.

"Oh, all right." Ginnie made her voice sound as if it didn't matter whether she did or not. She sat down and opened her little package.

"Would you like a cookie?" she asked.

"Oh—thanks! Gee!" Anna slowly bit into

the cookie. "Mm! Chocolate! Nuts! This is the best cookie I ever ate!"

"They're brownies," Ginnie told her. "My mother made them. Doesn't your mother know how to make brownies?"

Anna shook her head. "I haven't got a mother. She's dead. I live in the Home."

Ginnie looked up, shocked. An orphan! She had seen the Home, a big gray building on the edge of town.

"I just came there this summer," Anna explained. "I was in the Home over in Springfield. Only it was crowded, so they sent me here."

Ginnie was interested. "Then are you new in school?"

Anna nodded. "You are too, I know."

How awful, Ginnie thought, not to have any mother and father. She bit into a brownie thoughtfully.

"Don't you like to play tag?" Anna asked.

"No," Ginnie said.

"Don't you like games?"

"No. I hate them."

Anna looked at her in surprise. "I don't. I love to play games. We have a playground at the Home."

"Then why don't you go and play?" Ginnie didn't sound very friendly, she knew. For just a minute she had thought maybe . . . maybe she had found a friend. Now Anna wanted to play tag.

"I don't want to," Anna said, "because that Geneva—I don't think she likes me."

Ginnie remembered Geneva copying Anna as she wrote her composition.

"She didn't ask me to play," Anna said.

Ginnie was suddenly angrier than ever with Geneva. "Well, if you want to play . . ." she said.

"Oh, I don't!" Anna said quickly. "I'd much rather stay here with you."

Warmth flowed inside Ginnie. Anna was nice. How dared Geneva be mean to her—when Anna had no mother and father!

"What's it like in the Home?" she asked.

"Oh, it's real nice!" Anna seemed eager to have Ginnie believe that. "The Matron is a very nice lady. I help take care of the darling little babies. The only thing . . ." Anna hesitated.

"What?" Ginnie prompted.

Anna looked down at her clean, faded brown dress. "We don't have very nice clothes to wear. The big girls—sometimes they get a new dress. But I never. I get the ones the big girls outgrow."

Anna sighed. Then she looked up and the shy smile flashed out. "But I don't really mind!" Anna assured Ginnie.

The bell rang. They stood up.

"We can spend recess together every day!" Anna said. "I can give you half of my apple when I have one. Sometimes we have a whole barrel of apples," she explained proudly.

Ginnie wanted to make Anna happy. "That will be nice," she said. "I love apples."

Anna's brown eyes shone. "We'll be friends," she said. "Won't we, Georgina?"

Ginnie nodded. The nice warm feeling was spreading all through her now. Suddenly she cared nothing about Geneva and the others.

"Yes," Ginnie said, "we'll be friends!"

BIRTHDAY PARTY ON SATURDAY

Marjorie was going to have a birthday party Saturday afternoon. Ginnie spied her invitation, in the shape of an orange pumpkin, before she had reached her seat Monday morning. She glanced around. There was an invitation on every girl's desk.

It was October now, and chilly. This morning the radiators in the schoolroom thumped and hissed and sent out a smell of scorching iron with the welcome warmth.

Ginnie read her invitation, looked at the pumpkin, and read the invitation again. A pleasant tingle of excitement mixed with a feeling of dread.

She had never been to a party. She had only read about them. At parties you pinned the tail on the donkey and hunted for peanuts. Sometimes there was even a magician to do tricks. How exciting to be going to a real party!

On the other hand, she had a sinking feeling when she thought of having to play games with Geneva and all those other girls. It almost seemed as if she couldn't!

But Anna would be there. Ginnie glanced over at her friend. There was color in Anna's cheeks and her brown eyes were sparkling. She turned and caught Ginnie's eye and held up her invitation. Ginnie smiled back. Anna was thrilled, she could see.

At recess, Ginnie and Anna talked about the party.

"Oh," Anna said excitedly, "parties are lots of fun! We have parties at the Home. The Committee Ladies come and bring us candy and ice cream. Sometimes we have movies, even."

Ginnie was interested. "Do you have peanut hunts and magicians at your parties?"

Anna shook her head. "No." She considered. "I guess that's when you're invited to a party at a girl's house. Maybe we'll have those at Marjorie's party, huh?"

Ginnie nodded. "I guess so."

"And maybe we'll even have snappers, with hats and prizes in them! Once," Anna remembered, "we had those at the Home in Springfield. I got an orange hat. And a tiny, tiny horse. I've still got him! He's made of silver," she assured Ginnie.

Ginnie was impressed.

"And I guess we'll have little paper baskets with candy in them," Anna went on happily. "I know they have those at girls' parties. We never had them at the Home, though." Anna clasped her hands. "Oh, Georgina, aren't you glad we're invited to a party?"

Ginnie glanced at her friend. She had never seen Anna like this. She felt a little excited and curious about the party too, but not nearly as excited as Anna.

31

"Aren't you excited? Aren't you?" Anna insisted.

"Oh, yes!" Ginnie said.

The bell rang and they headed slowly toward the entrance. Just as they reached it there was a sudden mad rush around them. Geneva and the other tag-players arrived. The girls were laughing and out of breath.

Ginnie turned away, pretending not to see them.

"Hey, kids!" Geneva was shouting. "Let's decide. Are we going to or not?"

"Yes!" several voices shouted back.

"O.K.," Geneva said. She looked around the group that now included Ginnie and Anna. "Then the rule is that everybody's got to wear a new dress to Marjorie's party!"

Ginnie turned around suddenly.

"Will you wear a new dress?" Geneva was pointing her finger at one of the girls.

"Yes," the girl said obediently.

"Will you wear a new dress?" Geneva was going around the circle.

"Yes."

Geneva was coming to Anna. "Will you wear a new dress?" she demanded.

Ginnie took one look at Anna's face and moved quickly toward her.

"Will you?" Geneva insisted.

"I—I can't," Anna said.

Geneva stamped her foot. "There! You're the first one to spoil it!"

Ginnie tried to speak.

Geneva put her hands on her hips and stood facing Anna. "You can't go to Marjorie's party if you don't wear a new dress. So there!"

Marjorie's voice spoke up, protesting. "Oh, Geneva!"

"She can't. It's not allowed. We made a rule," Geneva said loudly.

But Anna turned away and went stumbling up the steps into the school.

Then, suddenly, Ginnie found her voice.

"Geneva Porter!" Ginnie cried, fury rising in her. "You keep still! Keep still! Do you hear?" Ginnie stamped her foot.

Geneva's jaw dropped.

Ginnie was too angry to care what she did. She faced Geneva. "Don't you know," she cried, "that Anna lives in the Home? Don't you know she hasn't any father or mother or any new clothes? Don't you know that?"

Even in her rage, Ginnie could see the color drain from Geneva's pink cheeks.

"You're a mean, hateful, horrible girl!" Ginnie went on.

Her fists were clenched. She didn't care. She could have hit Geneva! She didn't care that a bigger crowd had gathered. Dimly she heard the second bell. It meant nothing.

"You are the meanest, meanest, meanest girl in the world!" Ginnie said distinctly.

Geneva slowly lifted her head. She was not as tall as Ginnie. But something inside Ginnie wanted to step back. She did not step back.

"No," Geneva said, "I didn't know."

Ginnie had a strange feeling, almost a feeling of horror, as big tears suddenly rose to Geneva's eyes and rolled down her cheeks.

"Don't you talk to me like that!" Geneva said. "You just shut up yourself. Do you hear?"

They stood facing each other, both furious.

"I will not shut up!" Ginnie said.

"Come on, girls." It was a teacher. "Don't you know the second bell's rung?"

Ginnie turned away and stalked into school alone. Anna was in her seat. She had the top of her desk up and her face was hidden.

Anger still burned in Ginnie. Her thoughts were in a tumult. Anna wouldn't go to the party now. She wouldn't go herself, either. Of course it wasn't Geneva's party. It was Marjorie's. But no, she wouldn't go.

The class was subdued the rest of the morning. Geneva, who usually bounced about like a rubber ball, kept her eyes on her work and was strangely quiet.

At noon Anna didn't wait for Ginnie. Ginnie walked home alone. She was glad she had talked that way to Geneva. She knew how Anna was feeling—as if Geneva had slapped her in the face. Anna had been so excited, so eager about the party. Ginnie's heart ached.

Maybe she could make it up to her. Maybe Mother and Daddy would take them somewhere Saturday. Or maybe Mother would let her ask Anna to lunch. She had never had a friend to lunch. But she said nothing to Mother this noon. Mother wouldn't understand. She didn't know about Geneva and how mean she was.

"Georgina, I'm awfully sorry about this morning," Marjorie began. "It was all Geneva's idea about the new dresses. Honest. She thought it would be fun. But please don't pay any attention! You're coming to my party, aren't you? We're not going to wear new dresses. And make Anna come too, Please!"

Ginnie looked down at the ground. "I don't know whether I can. Maybe Anna will come, I don't know."

That afternoon the sky darkened and sheets of driving rain fell. Anna's seat was empty. Geneva kept her eyes straight ahead or on her desk.

Suddenly Ginnie gave a little jump. A folded note had thudded on her desk. She glanced around quickly. Geneva's head was bent over her work.

Ginnie hesitated. Should she open it? Was it something else mean? She slipped the note under her desk, braced herself for what was coming, and began undoing the wad of paper.

But it was nothing mean.

"I'm sorry," the note said. "I'll tell Anna I'm sorry, too. Can you come over to my house after school? Geneva."

Ginnie looked up in bewilderment. Then she set her lips. Slowly, but so Geneva could see, she tore the note to bits and went back to her work.

Half an hour later the second note landed.

"Are you still mad?" this note said.

Hot anger flowed over Ginnie. "Yes, I am!" she wanted to say. But she wouldn't give Geneva the satisfaction of knowing she was still upset. She tossed her head and threw the note in her desk.

The third note arrived near closing time.

"I am very sorry," it said. "Please do not be mad at me any more because I did not know about Anna. I will make it up. If you can't come to my house, how about me coming to your house? Love from your friend, Geneva."

For the first time Ginnie wavered. "Your

friend, Geneva." There was something about that that softened her heart a little. Could it be that Geneva was honestly trying to be nice? Ginnie picked up her pencil slowly, then laid it down.

Finally she tore a sheet from her pad, softly so Miss Roberts wouldn't hear. She picked up her pencil again. She wrote slowly, "You can come over if you want to," and tossed the note to Geneva.

Geneva turned and nodded hard, beaming at her.

Dismay began to creep over Ginnie. She didn't want Geneva! She didn't like her. Geneva was a mean girl. What would they do? What would Mother say? Ginnie felt so flustered she hardly knew what she was doing the rest of the afternoon.

Maybe, she thought hopefully, Geneva will remember something she has to do, and not come.

A NEW FRIEND

But when school was out, Geneva matter-of-factly tramped along beside Ginnie. "I can call up my mother from your house," Geneva said. She had recovered her poise. She did not mention what had happened, but she seemed to be making a special effort to be friendly.

Ginnie said nothing as they walked along. The rain had stopped. Geneva's hand slapped the ball she was bouncing along the wet, leaf-plastered pavement. "Have you got any brothers and sisters, Georgina?" she asked.

"No."

"Oh. Neither have I."

Geneva sounded—not mean this time, just disappointed. Ginnie felt she hadn't lived up to what Geneva had hoped.

"I've got a cat though," Ginnie said suddenly. Then she stopped, fully expecting Geneva to make a face at the thought of a mere cat.

"Oh, goody!" Geneva gave a skip. "I love cats!"

They walked on in silence. Ginnie didn't know what else to say.

Bounce, bounce! Geneva was concentrating on her ball as if that were the most important thing in the world. "We're not going to wear new dresses to Marjorie's party," she remarked, as if she had just thought of it.

Ginnie said nothing.

"But I thought," Geneva went on, "that maybe we could get Anna . . . I mean . . . I've got a new green sweater and skirt I've never worn. I want to give them to her!"

Ginnie looked at her in surprise. This was a new side of Geneva.

40

"Do you think she'd take them?" Geneva had stopped bouncing her ball now and was appealing to Ginnie seriously.

Ginnie considered. "I don't know. I don't think I would after . . . after . . ."

Geneva broke in. "But I didn't mean to hurt her feelings! I didn't know she lived in the Home!"

"But you oughtn't to say such things!"

Tears rose to Geneva's eyes again. "I know, but I didn't think! And I want to make it up to her and you won't help!"

Ginnie's heart melted. "Yes, I will!" she said hastily. "I'll help you."

"Oh, good!" Geneva was happy again.

Mother seemed a little surprised, but she said she was glad to see Geneva.

"Where is the cat?" Geneva demanded.

Mumbo was where she usually was in the afternoon, curled up on a chair in the dining room where the sunshine fell, if there was sunshine.

The little cat stretched out lazy, black silk paws and opened her pink mouth in a huge yawn.

Geneva got down on her knees and stroked Mumbo's head.

"Oh, you darling kitty," she murmured. "You darling, darling kitty!" Mumbo sat up, shook herself, and stared out the window, pretending to be bored.

Ginnie scooped her cat over her shoulder, burying her face in the clean, fresh-smelling fur. She was pleased that Geneva liked Mumbo. "I'll dress her up," she said. "I put my doll clothes on her and she looks so sweet. Just like a darling little monkey."

"First you'd better have something to eat," Mother said. "I've got a fresh chocolate cake. Get some glasses for milk, Ginnie dear."

Geneva sat at the kitchen table, eating happily and looking around the spotless red and white kitchen with interest. Mother talked to Geneva. Ginnie ate her cake and listened to the conversation.

Geneva tipped back her head and finished the milk. She pulled off her napkin. "Good!" she said. She looked at Mother, then at Ginnie. "Would your mother help us about Anna, Ginnie?" she asked.

Her nickname had a sweet, friendly sound. Ginnie felt a little thrill of happiness. "I didn't tell her," she said. "You tell her now."

Mother listened to Geneva's story. Then she looked thoughtfully at the two girls. "I think it would be very nice," she said. "Only you must do it the right way. I think, Ginnie, that you should write Anna a little note, telling her you missed her this afternoon. And you, Geneva"—Mother looked squarely at her—"must write too, telling her you're sorry you were thoughtless and unkind. And then you can both tell her you want her to have some things that you are sending. Are you sure your mother will want you to give up the green sweater and skirt, Geneva?"

"Oh, sure! If I want to," Geneva assured her.

"And, Ginnie, are you going to send Anna a little present?"

Ginnie had been thinking. She drew a long breath, making up her mind. "I know," she said. "My charm bracelet. And my new green ribbons."

The charm bracelet was her favorite piece

43

of jewelry. Mother looked at her. "All right," Mother said, and smiled.

They decided to write the notes now.

"Ginnie's daddy can take the notes and the things over tonight," Mother said. "He can pick up the sweater and skirt at your house, Geneva."

They wrote the notes up in Ginnie's room, sitting on opposite sides of the little table that Ginnie used as a desk.

"There!" Geneva put down the pen. "Mine's done."

"Mine too." Ginnie signed her name.

"Let's see."

They exchanged letters.

"Dearest Anna," Ginnie had written. "I missed you very much this afternoon. I am sending you a little present. Please come to school tomorrow. Love from your friend Georgina."

Geneva had written: "Dearest Anna, I am very mad at myself because I didn't mean to be mean to you and I was. Will you please forgive me. I feel terrible. I think you are swell and I hope you will play tag. I hope

you will come to the party and come to my
house to play too. Nobody is going to wear
any old new dresses to Marjorie's party. Here
is something for you from me, not for the
party but for any old time. (In the package.)
Love and kisses from your friend Geneva."

"There!" Geneva licked her envelope and
pressed down the flap. "That's done!" She
gave a sigh of relief. Then she glanced around
the room. "I'm going to look at your books."

Ginnie's books filled two low shelves along
the wall of her room. She loved them and
she loved having a place for them at last.
Some day she was going to have a room with
bookshelves way to the ceiling.

Geneva had flopped on the floor and was
looking along the shelves. "I've read this and
this and this." Her finger tapped the backs
of the books. "Do you read a lot, Ginnie?"

Ginnie nodded.

"So do I. Only not when I can go out and
play or something." Geneva scrambled up and
looked out the window. "Let's go out and play
ball."

Ginnie followed. So Geneva had read a lot

of books, too. Why, she thought, Geneva is smart!

It was damp and chilly in the gray afternoon. Ginnie and Geneva bounced their balls hard, seeing who could count the farthest. Geneva stopped to rest. She looked over at the house next door.

"Say," she said, "isn't that where Peter lives?"

Ginnie nodded.

"Let's call him," Geneva suggested.

Ginnie considered. She'd never think of calling to Peter herself. In fact, even after all this time she had never spoken to him. But if Geneva wanted to . . . Ginnie felt rather excited at the idea of Peter coming over.

Just then the back door of Peter's house slammed. Both girls looked up. Peter was coming down the steps. Pattering ahead of him was his golden cocker spaniel.

"Hi, Peter!" Geneva shouted.

Peter stopped suddenly, raised his head, and looked over. Even from here they could see the startled expression on his face. Then he turned hastily and went back in, slamming the door again.

Ginnie's heart sank. Peter didn't want to come over. He didn't like her. Well, of course he didn't, she thought. Boys liked girls who laughed and were good at games. Not girls who couldn't even play tag!

Geneva put her hands on her hips. "Well! See if we care if he doesn't want to play with us!" She made a face. "Look, this is Peter!"

Ginnie couldn't keep from smiling. Geneva was funny, all right, when she was copying someone else.

Ginnie shivered and turned her back on Peter's house. "Let's go in," she said, "and dress Mumbo."

At five o'clock they were still sitting on the floor, giggling over Mumbo in her long white dress and frilled bonnet. Mumbo sat motionless where Ginnie put her, her small black face solemn and her yellow eyes round.

"She thinks she can't move when she's dressed up!" Ginnie giggled.

Geneva grabbed the little cat and hugged

her. She put her down and Mumbo sat like a statue of a cat. They both giggled again. Geneva rolled over on the floor.

"Oh, dear!" She sat up and sighed happily. "We're having fun! But I guess I've got to go home."

Ginnie and Mother went to the front door.

"You've got to come over to my house, Ginnie," Geneva said. "Can she come tomorrow?" she asked Mother.

The thought of going to a strange house— Geneva's house—sent a chill up Ginnie's spine.

"We'll see," Mother said. "But Ginnie's father will come for the sweater and skirt tonight after supper." Mother hesitated. "Maybe I'd better talk to your mother on the phone first."

"O.K.," Geneva said. "You'll like my mother though." She looked up in Mother's face.

Mother smiled. Suddenly, she put her arm around Geneva and gave her a squeeze. "I know I'll like her, dear. And I'm glad you're Ginnie's friend."

Ginnie followed Mother slowly away from the door. Her friend! Was Geneva really her friend? Geneva hadn't been mean once all afternoon. And she was kind and generous. She wanted to make up to Anna for being so mean. Could it possibly be that she had misjudged Geneva?

When Daddy heard the story of Anna at the dinner table, he said, "Why, sure. I'll be your messenger boy."

Ginnie went along and waited in the car while Daddy got the box with the skirt and sweater at Geneva's house and delivered the presents and the notes they had written to the Home.

The next morning Anna was in school. She was not wearing the new sweater and skirt. But she was smiling.

At recess both Ginnie and Geneva anxiously waited for Anna.

"I got the letters. And the presents," Anna said, beaming at them. "Gee, I never had anything so pretty! Thank you!"

"Aren't you going to wear them?" Geneva demanded.

Anna nodded. "I'm saving them—for the party."

Ginnie's breath caught with relief. Then everything was all right.!

"That's swell!" Geneva hopped up and down. "Come on, kids," she cried. "Let's get into the tag game."

Ginnie hesitated a moment. "Come on, Anna," she said. She held out her hand.

The two girls raced over the playground after Geneva.

AT GENEVA'S HOUSE

The weeks passed swiftly. Ginnie was beginning to look forward to school now. She went to Geneva's house or Geneva came to hers almost every afternoon.

Sometimes Anna came too. But usually Anna went back to the Home to help mind the babies.

Ginnie played tag every recess now. At first she was terrified for fear she wouldn't be able to catch anyone. Or if she did, that someone would tag her right back. Fear lent speed to her feet.

"Hey," Geneva said, "you're a good player!"

GINNIE AND GENEVA

Ginnie ran faster. Her legs were long, and she turned out to be one of the best runners in the class. It was wonderful and astonishing to be a good player!

On this particular day, late in October, Geneva had a music lesson. Ginnie and Anna walked as far as they could together. Then Ginnie went on alone. She hummed as she skipped along, swinging her books in their bag. It was a beautiful afternoon. The sky was vivid blue. The trees tossed their branches. And it was Friday!

She came in sight of the white house. Ginnie scanned the window for Mother. But today Mother wasn't watching. She wasn't at the door either. That was strange, because she always heard Ginnie's step.

There were voices upstairs when Ginnie opened the door. Who could it be? She stood doubtfully, listening. She slipped off her coat. As she turned to hang it in the hall closet, a yellow paper on the table caught her eye. She looked again. A telegram!

Ginnie peered at it, her coat half off. The words were printed and plain. YOUR MOTHER

52

VERY ILL. COME IF POSSIBLE. DR. LUTHER
JONES.

It took Ginnie a second to get the meaning. Now she saw that the telegram was ad-
dressed to Mrs. Richard Fellows. Why, it must
mean Grandma. Grandma was sick!

Mother appeared at the top of the stairs.
She had her hat on. "Oh, darling," Mother
cried, "I didn't hear you come in!"

"I . . . I saw the telegram," Ginnie said.

Mother came downstairs. "Ginnie, I've got
to go away. Daddy will be here any minute."

Ginnie looked up in her face. "Can't I go
too?"

Mother shook her head. "No, dear. Daddy's going with me. We're taking the train to
the city and flying from there." She sat down
and drew Ginnie toward her. "You're going
to stay at Geneva's. Won't that be fun! Her
mother is here now to take you there."

It all happened so quickly. The drive to
the station in Mrs. Porter's car. The train
roaring in.

"Have a good time with Geneva, darling,"
Mother said.

"Be good, monkey." Daddy's arm was tight around her. "Maybe there'll be a present when we come home."

The train chugged, moved. Mother and Daddy were waving. Then the chugging died away in the distance.

"Well, they're off," Mrs. Porter said cheerfully, her arm around Ginnie's shoulders. "Won't Geneva be surprised to know you're going to visit her!"

Mumbo was looking out of the car window with startled yellow eyes. Mumbo was going to Geneva's too.

"I don't know what Geneva's daddy will say," Mrs. Porter remarked. "He doesn't like cats."

"He'll be nice to her though, won't he?" Geneva asked anxiously.

Mrs. Porter laughed. "He'll sputter. Then he'll probably sneak her a dish of salmon when I'm not looking."

Driving to Geneva's, Ginnie couldn't speak through the ache in her throat. Already she missed Mother and Daddy so much! She'd never stayed away from Mother all night before.

As the tires crackled on the gravel driveway, Geneva's surprised face appeared at the window, then disappeared. Geneva came to the door. Mrs. Porter took Ginnie's suitcase and they went in.

"Surprise!" Mrs. Porter beamed at her daughter.

Geneva stood, hands on hips. "Hey, what is this?"

Ginnie giggled in spite of herself. "I'm going to visit you, Geneva, because my mother and daddy had to go see my grandma. She's sick. And I've got my clothes and everything."

"How long?" Geneva demanded, taking Mumbo.

"We don't know," Mrs. Porter said. "But just as long as she needs to stay we'll love to have her."

"Yes!" Geneva spun around, holding the cat. "Oh, goody, goody! I'm glad they've gone. Boy, we'll have fun!" She stopped spinning. "I didn't mean I'm glad your grandma's sick!"

She looked so sorry Ginnie couldn't help laughing. Geneva laughed too. Mrs. Porter was smiling as she carried Ginnie's suitcase upstairs.

"Now," Mrs. Porter said, after Ginnie and Geneva had had a glass of cider, "let's talk over what we're going to do this weekend."

Geneva's mother had white hair, though she wasn't old, and the bluest eyes Ginnie had ever seen. When she smiled, it seemed to Ginnie a dazzling light had been turned on.

Now the blue eyes were exclamation points as Mrs. Porter looked at Ginnie. "Your first real visit with us! The first of many, we hope, don't we, Geneva?"

Geneva nodded. "Sure. Lucy and Leonard are coming over tonight to play card games. I asked them."

"Oh, you did!" Mrs. Porter looked amused but pleased with her daughter for making her own arrangements.

Lucy and Leonard Ransom were the twins in their class. They lived down the street from Geneva. Lucy had dark, curly hair. Ginnie thought she was very pretty. But Leonard. Oh, dear! Leonard didn't like her, Ginnie was sure, any more than Peter did. Besides, when other children were around, Geneva wasn't as nice as when they played alone.

"I don't know any card games," Ginnie said nervously. If only they'd let her stay upstairs and read!

"Oh, they'll teach you," Geneva's mother told her.

Ginnie felt trapped. She wished she were safe at home.

But at suppertime Geneva's house was a merry place. The bright, warm kitchen. The good baked-potato smell. The crisp, juicy sputter of lamb chops when Mrs. Porter pulled out the broiler.

Mr. Porter came in.

"Good!" he said, welcoming Ginnie. "We need another girl around here!" But he just grunted at Mumbo.

Supper was fun, even if Ginnie did have a sick feeling when she thought of the evening ahead. Geneva and her mother joked and teased each other. They teased Mr. Porter.

57

Ginnie began to giggle. Geneva looked at her, then leaned over and whispered to her mother.

"Know what I told her?" Geneva demanded.

Ginnie shook her head. The old uncomfortable fear of Geneva crept back.

"I said you looked almost pretty."

Ginnie's eyes flew wide. She felt her cheeks flush.

"You do look pretty!" Geneva cried.

"Quiet," Mr. Porter said.

"It's rude to comment on people's looks," Mrs. Porter told her daughter. Her cornflower eyes danced at Ginnie. "But you really do," she added.

Ginnie looked from one to the other. She wasn't pretty, she knew, yet . . .

"You're pretty when you smile. Smile a lot, Ginnie," Geneva's mother told her.

They were doing the dishes when Mrs. Porter looked up, her hands busy in the suds, and said, "Ginnie and Jennie! I've got twins! The Ransoms aren't the only ones!"

Geneva flapped her towel. "Don't you call

me Jennie! Geneva's a bad enough name, but I just can't stand Jennie."

"She was named for my sister Jennie," Mrs. Porter told Ginnie, ignoring her child, "and my sister Lizzie. Only instead of being Jennie Lizzie, she's Geneva Elizabeth. And the ungrateful wretch doesn't like her beautiful name. So if she gets fresh, just call her Jennie!"

Ginnie couldn't imagine calling Geneva Jennie. No telling how Geneva might get back. But she stored the name away in her mind.

There was a stamping on the porch and the Ransoms burst in.

"Hello, Mrs. Porter, hello, Geneva, hello, Ginnie," they said almost together.

"Hi!" Geneva danced around them with her towel.

Lucy smiled at Ginnie, and Ginnie managed a shy smile of greeting.

They played a card game. Ginnie struggled to understand, and her head was beginning to ache with the effort when Leonard threw his cards on the table.

"Who wants to play dumb card games!" he said. "Let's do something else."

"What shall we do?" Lucy asked.

"I know!" Geneva said. "Let's make fudge."

Mr. and Mrs. Porter had gone out. But Geneva said she knew how to make fudge. "You dump in a lot of sugar and milk and chocolate and butter, and cook it till it makes a ball in water," she said.

Geneva got out the pan. Lucy measured the sugar. "Put in plenty," Leonard said, watching her. Ginnie brought the butter and milk from the refrigerator.

"Are you sure you put in enough sugar?" Leonard asked.

Lucy dumped in some more. "There! I spilled some," she said. "Shall I use all this milk?"

Geneva was getting the chocolate. "Oh, sure," she said. "Get another bottle out. We want a lot of fudge."

They set the fudge on the burner to cook.

"Now we just stir it sometimes and don't let it boil too hard," Geneva said. She had an apron tied under her arms and a big spoon in her hand. Geneva could do everything, Ginnie thought!

They stood around, waiting for the fudge to boil.

"Geneva," Lucy said, "remember that time in kindergarten when you had the whole class to a party?"

Ginnie looked from one to another as they talked about things they had done in the other grades. She wished she could join in. She felt lonely and left out.

"Fudge's boiling," Geneva sang out, and lowered the gas. "Now it won't be long."

"Gee, that smells good!" Leonard sniffed. He walked over to look, his feet crunching on the spilled sugar.

"Don't walk on the sugar," Lucy said.

"I'll try the fudge now," Geneva decided. She dripped some of the brown liquid into a cup of cold water. "Still soft."

The fudge boiled and boiled, but every time they tried it in cold water it ran all over the bottom of the cup.

Leonard went to look again. "You ought to turn up the gas."

"No! It'll burn." Geneva was positive.

"It's never going to cook," Leonard declared.

61

"I'll turn it up a little," Geneva said.

"Don't squnch in the sugar!" Lucy begged.

"I like to squnch in it." Leonard lifted his feet and put them down with a grinding sound.

"Stop!" Geneva shouted. "It gives me the shivers!"

"Oh, O.K." Leonard walked out of the sugar, but he still squnched. "It's stuck on," he said.

"Wipe it off," Lucy told him.

Leonard grabbed a crumpled piece of paper from the table and wiped the soles of his shoes.

"Hey, that's what I greased the pan with!" Geneva cried.

"Oh. Well, that's O.K.," Leonard said. "I like butter and sugar." He wiped a finger across the sole of his shoe.

Lucy and Geneva pounced on him. "Don't you lick it!" Lucy screeched.

"And take off your shoes before you get my mother's floor all greasy!" Geneva ordered.

"The fudge, the fudge! It's boiling over!" Ginnie cried.

The brown bubbles rose. Lucy squealed.

Leonard shouted, "Hey, look out!"

With a hissing sound the fudge foamed over the edge of the pan.

Geneva yelled and jumped to turn down the gas. The bubbles shrank quickly back. But a good share of their fudge was a sticky, light-brown mess on the stove.

"I ought to make you clean this up, Leonard Ransom!" Geneva said as she got the dishcloth.

Leonard padded over in his stocking feet. "Nope. That's girls' work. Hey, why don't you scrape it up and put it back in the pan?"

The girls shouted at him. "No!"

"O.K., O.K.," Leonard said. He peered in the pan. "There's plenty left, anyhow. I'll beat it. That'll make it get done."

"It had better get done pretty soon," Lucy said, looking at the clock, "because we've got to go home."

Leonard beat and beat. "This slop's never going to get thick," he said finally.

"Oh, dear, what'll we do?" Geneva wailed.

63

"I'm so hungry for a piece of fudge!" Lucy said.

Ginnie said nothing. She had been looking forward to that first warm, smooth, chocolaty piece.

"Well, we might as well throw this out," Leonard said. "I bet you didn't put in enough sugar, that's what's the matter."

Just then Mrs. Porter came in. "What's going on here?" she inquired.

"Leonard's beating the fudge," Geneva told her, "but it *won't* get hard!"

"Does he always take his shoes off to beat fudge?" Mrs. Porter asked. "How much milk did you use?"

"Only a bottle and a half."

"Heavens! You'd need a couple of pounds of sugar to make fudge of that!"

"I told you you didn't put in enough sugar," Leonard said.

They looked dismayed. "But we're starving," Geneva said.

Mrs. Porter was opening the refrigerator. "Well, we'll try and make something out of this. It's going to be pretty sweet." She poured in some more milk and put the pan back on the stove.

Five minutes later she poured steaming cups of cocoa.

Ginnie tasted her cocoa. It was sweet, all right. Geneva tasted hers. "Too sweet!" she exclaimed. Lucy made a small face.

Leonard tasted his. He smacked his lips. "Yummy! Could I have some more sugar, please?"

As the twins left, Leonard said, "That was the best fudge I ever drank!"

The girls finally got into the twin beds in Geneva's room. Ginnie stretched out in the dark.

It hadn't been so bad, having the twins there. They were nice. Ginnie was keyed up from the evening's excitement. Suddenly she felt like talking. She couldn't talk to Geneva about things that had happened in school. But lots of funny things had happened to her and Mother and Daddy. She wanted to tell about them.

Geneva was fun to talk to. Ginnie could feel her listening, and her laugh bubbled out

65

of the dark. Ginnie began to tell about the time her hat blew off and landed on Daddy's head.

Mrs. Porter came to the door. "Ginnie and Jennie, the gigglers!" she said. "Don't you know it's late?"

They giggled again. "We can't help it," Geneva said. "Oh, you're so funny, Ginnie! What else happened?"

Ginnie was really wound up. "Oh, I remember something!" she said. "It's awful funny!" She had barely started when they were all in gales of laughter.

Ginnie awoke to a room full of dancing sunshine and the crisp scurry of leaves outdoors. She glanced across at Geneva's bed. Geneva was still asleep, her dark head deep in the blanket.

Ginnie lay thinking dreamily. A long time ago she had thought Geneva was mean. Now Geneva seemed the friendliest, funniest, nicest friend anyone could have. Ginnie sighed. She wished she could be funny and popular and have loads of friends, like Geneva.

After breakfast Geneva got out her roller skates and Lucy came over with hers. Ginnie sat on the step and watched.

"Haven't you got any skates, Ginnie?" Lucy asked.

Ginnie shook her head.

"You can borrow mine," Geneva told her. "It's easy. Want to try?"

"No, thank you," Ginnie said.

She was sure she could never learn to skate. She couldn't bear to try, with the kids looking at her. But it did look like fun. She watched the two girls as they sped toward her laughing, arms outstretched. The loud scratch of the wheels on the pavement was a good sound.

"Come on, try," Lucy coaxed.

But Ginnie shook her head. She'd look silly.

IN THE BUSHEL BASKET

Grandma was going to get well. But she was still very weak. So Mother had to stay. Already Mother had been gone three weeks. Daddy came to see Ginnie on two weekends. He brought her the present he had promised—a little gold necklace—and one just like it for Geneva. Then he started off on a business trip.

Sometimes Ginnie cried a little at bedtime, missing Mother, but by morning she forgot to be homesick and went happily along to school with Geneva.

The early November days were excitingly

beautiful. The winds had stripped most of the trees bare, and swept the sky to a clear, fresh blue. White frost sparkled on the roofs and turned to silver the thick, dry leaves blanketing every yard. The whiff of wood smoke hung in the air.

Ginnie and Geneva, waiting for Lucy and Leonard to catch up one morning, hopped up and down in front of the house to keep warm.

"Hurry up!" Ginnie called, her teeth chattering. "We're f-freezing!"

"Hey!" Geneva was looking toward the front steps. "There's that old cat under our porch again."

The cat was apparently a stray. He had been slipping in and out under the porch for several days. "Poor kitty," Ginnie said. "He prob'ly hasn't got any home."

The four children hurried along together. Ginnie wondered briefly if the strange cat had anything to eat.

Miss Roberts had an announcement to make this morning. The eys of 4-B were on her expectantly. "I want to tell you," Miss Roberts said, "about something very important which will take place next June. There's going to be a school hobby show, and every child in the school may enter an exhibit."

Oh, dear, Ginnie thought. I haven't any hobby.

"Of course you won't be in my class then." Miss Roberts smiled at them. "But I want you to know now, so you can be thinking and planning about it. And of course if you have no hobby, this is the time to start one."

They discussed hobbies for a while. Several boys had model railroads. Peter had a stamp collection. Leonard had a chemistry set. John and Frederick had work benches and made things out of wood. Dorothy and Jane said their hobby was knitting. Marjorie said ice skating was hers.

Geneva wasn't sure she had a hobby. As for Ginnie, she shook her head when Miss Roberts asked her.

They discussed the hobby show, walking home from school. "Is reading a hobby?" Ginnie wanted to know.

"I think you have to *do* something for a hobby," Geneva replied. "Like making things."

"But what could we make?" Ginnie hated sewing. She didn't know how to knit. "We could have cooking for a hobby," she suggested.

"Yes." Geneva said, "and suppose we made fudge for the exhibit and it turned out to be cocoa!"

Ginnie giggled. They'd better not have cooking for a hobby.

"We could collect something." Geneva said thoughtfully.

"What could we collect?"

They turned into Geneva's front walk and Mumbo ran to meet them, purring a welcome. Ginnie picked her up. Out of the corner of her eye she saw the stray cat slip like a shadow around the corner of the house. Geneva ran after him, but the cat had disappeared.

Mrs. Porter opened the door for them.

"That cat's still around," Geneva said.

Mrs. Porter nodded. "I've driven him away and driven him away. He looks hungry, poor thing, but if we feed him he'll never go."

"Oh," Ginnie said, "poor hungry cat!"

71

"I know," Mrs. Porter said. "But you know how Geneva's father feels about cats. He just tolerates Mumbo."

Ginnie tried to forget the stray cat. But when she went out to play, the cat was sitting on the front walk. Before he slipped under the porch again his eyes searched Ginnie's with a pleading look that nearly broke her heart.

Oh, the poor, poor cat without any home! She waited for a few minutes, but he didn't come back.

At supper they discussed the hobby show with Mrs. Porter. Mr. Porter was off on business for a few days.

"It would be fine for both of you to have a hobby," Mrs. Porter said. "Hobbies are fun and they teach you things you'll never learn in school. Why don't you start some sort of collection?"

"We can't think of anything to collect!" Then Geneva's face brightened. "We could collect wild flowers! I know a good place for violets."

"Not this time of year, child," her mother said. "But you know what? I believe, if you asked him, Daddy would take you two on some hikes. You could begin to learn the plants and the trees and birds and rocks. He hasn't done that sort of thing for a long time," she added. "But if he had two little girls to go along, I believe you'd all have a wonderful time."

"A hike in the woods?" Ginnie asked doubtfully.

Mrs. Porter nodded.

"But there might be snakes."

"Oh, not in winter, Ginnie!" Geneva cried. "Snakes don't come out in winter."

Ginnie was not convinced. Ugh! She shuddered. But still, a hike might be fun. They grew more and more excited. They could hardly wait for Mr. Porter to come home the next night.

It was after school next day, when Ginnie and Geneva and the Ransom twins were playing hide-and-seek in the back yard, that Ginnie saw the stray cat again. He was running

73

along, close to the hedge, toward the open garage door. There was something strange about the cat's movements.

"Look," Ginnie said suddenly, her eyes following the cat. "He's got something in his mouth." Just then the cat disappeared inside the garage.

"I'm going to look!" Ginnie cried.

The other three followed. It was dim inside the garage, and Ginnie paused to look around. There was no sign of the cat.

Then a faint rustle came from the far end of the garage. It came from an old bushel basket. Ginnie walked toward it. Suddenly she was looking down at the stray cat. But that wasn't all. Ginnie gave a gasp. Cuddled up close beside the old cat were four of the tiniest kittens she had ever seen.

Geneva was right behind her, "Oh, the darling, darling baby kittens!"

"Are they alive?" Lucy whispered.

"Sure they're alive," Leonard said. "But look, they haven't even got their eyes open yet."

"She must have carried them in here from under the porch." Ginnie reached in. The old cat looked up beseechingly, but made no objection.

Ginnie put her hand in the warm, soft, furry mass and took up one of the tiny things. It was tiger-striped, its pink mouth open, its pink claws wide-stretched. She held it against her face. The soft baby thing!

Each child held a kitten while the mother watched anxiously.

"Oh, Geneva," Ginnie said suddenly, "we've just got to give the mother cat something to eat!"

Geneva nodded. "Sure we have! I'm going to tell Mother."

She dashed off, while the others hung admiringly over the basket. Geneva came back, carrying a saucer of milk. Mrs. Porter was with her.

"Well!" Mrs. Porter said to the mother cat. "So this is what you were up to. And I never guessed."

Geneva showed the mother cat the milk,

then put it down on the floor. The cat jumped down and lapped hungrily.

"What do you think your father will say?" Mrs. Porter asked Geneva. "He objects to having one cat. What's he going to say to five more?"

Ginnie and Geneva looked at each other and giggled.

"You'll have to break the news," Mrs. Porter declared, going into the house.

Mr. Porter got home in time for dinner. He stretched out wearily in a big chair. Mumbo jumped in his lap and he pushed her off. "Get out, cat." Then Mr. Porter looked at Mumbo. "Don't they give you enough to eat? You look kind of scrawny."

"Mumbo's just a little cat," Ginnie explained, picking her up.

"Shall I tell him now?" Geneva whispered to her mother.

"Wait till he's had dinner," her mother whispered back.

They had a very good dinner. Mr. Porter pushed back his pie plate with a contented sigh. "Well," he said, "I feel better."

Ginnie looked at Geneva and they both put up their hands to hide the smiles.

"I'm glad you feel better, Daddy," Geneva said, "because you're going to be awful mad."

Her father looked at her. "Now what?" he said.

"An old cat is in our garage," Geneva said, her eyes dancing. "And guess what she's got!"

"Oh, for heaven's sake!" Mr. Porter said.

Ginnie and Geneva laughed out loud. "Kittens!" Geneva cried. "Four!"

"And we've got to keep them," Ginnie added, "because they haven't any home!"

"Can we, Daddy? Can we?" Geneva bounced in her chair.

"We cannot," her father said.

"Oh-h!" Geneva wailed.

Ginnie said nothing, but her heart sank.

"Well, anyway," Mrs. Porter told them, "take Daddy out to see the kittens while I clear the table."

They traipsed out to the garage. It was a sharp night and Ginnie shivered in her sweater. Mr. Porter peered down, an expression of disgust on his face. The old cat looked up, studying him.

"Hold one, Daddy!" Geneva cried. She picked up a kitten and thrust the tiny, soft thing into her father's hands.

"I don't want to hold it," he said hastily. He pulled the kitten's claws from his coat. "Here, you, go back to your mother." He glanced down at the saucer.

"We gave her some milk," Geneva said apologetically.

"That's bad." Mr. Porter frowned and shook his head. "You'll never get rid of her if you feed her."

Ginnie was very unhappy as she helped wipe the dishes. What was going to become of those darling babies?

"Don't discuss it any more," Mrs. Porter said when Mr. Porter went into the other room. "Just wait a while."

At eight o'clock Ginnie and Geneva went up to bed. They were all undressed when Geneva said suddenly, "I'm hungry. I want a glass of milk."

They padded downstairs in their bare feet.

In the kitchen doorway they both stopped suddenly, Ginnie peering over Geneva's shoulder.

The back door stood open. And just going out of it was Mr. Porter. In one hand he held a steaming saucepan. Over his arm was an old sweater.

"What are you doing?" Geneva cried.

"What are *you* doing!" Mr. Porter said crossly, turning around. "I suppose you'd let your cats starve."

"Did you heat some milk?" Geneva asked in amazement.

"You can't give a cat cold milk on a night like this," her father retorted.

"What are you going to do with that sweater?" Ginnie inquired.

Mr. Porter looked down as if he had forgotten the sweater. "Oh, that. Well, they've got to have something to sleep on." He went out and banged the door.

Ginnie and Geneva looked at each other. Then Geneva turned and ran into the living room. "He does like them!" she cried. "Do you s'pose he'll let us keep them?"

Mrs. Porter's eyes were twinkling. "Did I hear you say," she inquired, "that you thought you'd collect wild flowers? Looks to me as if you're collecting something else."

"What?" Geneva demanded.

"Cats," said Mrs. Porter.

THE
WONDERFUL
DAY

But even with six cats to feed and keep out
from under Mr. Porter's feet, Ginnie and Geneva decided they needed another hobby.
They couldn't very well show six cats in the
hobby show.

Besides, when the cats began staggering
around, even they agreed that five cats besides Mumbo were too many. When the kittens were big enough to look after themselves,
they were going to find homes for them with
people who loved cats. They were taking or-
ders at school.

Geneva broached the subject of a hike to

her father. Collecting wild flowers and things appealed to them more than anything else.

"Sounds like a good idea," Mr. Porter said. "I'd like to get out in the woods myself."

"Oh, goody!" Geneva clapped her hands. "Can we go Saturday, Daddy?"

"I don't know why not. I've got a knapsack somewhere. We'll take our lunch."

"Lunch?" Ginnie was astonished. "In winter?"

"You wait," Mr. Porter told her. "This'll be the best picnic you ever went on."

Thursday night Geneva's father had a new idea. "Have you kids ever seen the sun come up out of doors?"

They shook their heads.

"How would you like to start before daylight?"

"Before *daylight?*" Geneva and Ginnie looked at each other in amazement.

"We'll cook our breakfast in the woods."

What a lark! The girls danced about the room, their arms around each other.

"You'll have to go to bed right after supper tomorrow night." Mrs. Porter told them.

Friday night they helped pack the knap-sack. There were cans of orange juice and evaporated milk, eggs and bacon, a coffee-cake, bread and butter and cheese, hot dogs and cookies. The knapsack held them all, along with the skillet and thermos bottle and plastic cups and plates and other things Mr. Porter said they'd need.

They were on their way to bed when Gin-nie, glancing from the window, gasped, "It's snowing!"

Sure enough, fine feathery flakes were sift-ing down under the street light.

"Oh," Geneva moaned, looking out. "Then we can't go?"

"Of course we can. This won't amount to much," her father said. "It's nice in the woods after a snow."

It seemed to Ginnie she had just closed her eyes when she heard someone calling. It was pitch dark.

"Hurry up!" Geneva was already putting on her clothes. She was shivering. "It's going to be daylight if you don't hurry."

83

Ginnie took time to peer through the window. It had stopped snowing and a light sprinkle of white lay over the ground.

When they went downstairs, Mrs. Porter met them in the lighted kitchen. "Here's some hot milk." The milk steamed as she poured it into three glasses. "This will warm you up and stay you till breakfast."

The warm glass felt good in Ginnie's cold hands. The hot milk made a warm path down her throat.

They got into snowsuits. Ginnie began to feel hot. When they stepped outdoors the air was cool and refreshing on her face. They spoke in whispers.

"Getting daylight." Mr. Porter pointed to the sky as they climbed into the car. "I'm afraid we won't see much of a sunrise. It's cloudy."

They drove through the silent streets and headed onto the highway. The heat in the car began to feel good on their feet.

It really was getting light now. Ginnie looked curiously at the houses and roadstands. How different they looked. How neat and uncluttered and deserted in the strange gray light.

"Sun's up," Mr. Porter said, peering out, "but it's behind a cloud."

The mist began to roll away and mountains rose around them. The road led along a winding river, silver in the early light. Traces of color lingered in the trees on the slopes. Over everything was the light, silvery powdering of snow.

Mr. Porter was watching now, looking for a place to turn. He swung off the highway onto a gravel road. Beside them the mountain rose steeply. Mr. Porter drew up to the side of the road. "Think you can climb this before breakfast?"

They could hardly wait to get out. Mr. Porter locked the car, shrugged into his knapsack, and they set off.

The path was steep. Ginnie stopped suddenly. "Look at all the tracks in the snow!"

The tracks crisscrossed the trail in every direction. Mr. Porter studied them. "Squirrel tracks, probably, and chipmunk, and—yes, here are deer tracks too."

Ginnie looked around in wonder.

They went up, up, and the woods closed all about them. Then, just as Ginnie was getting to feel starved, the sky was ahead and the path ended on a mass of rocks. Geneva, running ahead, called to them to hurry.

Far below stretched the valley, dotted here and there by white houses, red barns. Beyond, the hills rose in row upon distant row, fading to a shadow against the sky. As they stood, quiet, the tinkle of a cowbell drifted up, clear and sweet.

"Well"—Mr. Porter slipped the knapsack from his shoulders—"Here's where we eat. See if you can find a lot of dry twigs."

Ginnie watched, fascinated, as he made a hearth of three large stones and laid his fire of paper and twigs. The kindling caught, the small flame brightened and crackled and crept upward in a thin column of smoke. Mr. Porter broke larger pieces of branches and fed the fire.

"Now," he said, dusting his hands, "where's the food?"

The sweet, mouth-watering fragrance of

bacon sputtering in the skillet was delicious. Scrambled eggs tasting of wood smoke, steaming cocoa, toast and jam, had never been so good. The wind, here on the high rocks, was sharp and stung tears to their eyes. But the fire toasted their backs as they looked over the valley. The plates of food and cups of cocoa were warm in their hands.

"What's that?" Ginnie turned and raised her head. "Is that birds making that noise?"

"No." Mr. Porter looked up. "It sounds like gulls screaming, doesn't it? But it's trees, rubbing together in the wind."

The branches screamed. Dry leaves scurried to earth like flocks of small brown birds. Suddenly the sun came out. Its golden light crept along the ground under the trees till the whole forest was illuminated.

"Well," Mr. Porter said at last, beginning to gather the plates, "we'd better get along."

They wiped the dishes off as well as they could and packed everything neatly. Mr. Porter made sure the fire was out and the ashes scattered before they left.

They walked briskly, Mr. Porter first, Geneva next, Ginnie last. There was no snow here, deep in the woods. Dry leaves rustled under their feet, making a golden trail in the sunlight.

"Look!" Ginnie stopped. Small crimson berries lay at her feet.

"Take some home," Mr. Porter said. "Part of your hobby, you know, is to look these plants up and find out what they are."

Geneva made the next discovery. Hundreds of tiny Christmas trees only a few inches high. They took some of those along.

They found a plant that bore a small fruit, like tiny withered apples. There were ferns and mosses, dainty and delicate when you looked close. "You'll enjoy reading about mosses," Geneva's father told them.

More red berries. "Taste these," Mr. Porter said. He watched their faces. "It's wintergreen." Sure enough, the small, juicy berries had the tang of wintergreen gum!

The trail dipped into a broad valley. Mr. Porter looked over at a rocky pile some distance to their right. "I'd like to climb that and see what's on the other side," he said. "You kids want to wait for me here?"

"I want to go too!" Geneva cried.

"I think I'll wait," Ginnie decided. She had a sudden wish to hear how still it was when no one was around.

"You won't budge from this spot, will you," Mr. Porter instructed her.

Ginnie sat down on a fallen tree that lay across the trail. She watched the distant figures of Geneva and her father making their way up the rocks. Then they disappeared over the top.

How still, Ginnie thought. The silence was deep, yet there were many sounds in it—the snap of twig, boom of wind, gurgle of water. The stillness pounded on Ginnie's eardrums. She didn't move. She scarcely breathed, hating to break the quiet with a noise not of the woods.

Suddenly Ginnie turned her head. It was not something she had heard. It was more as if she felt a presence that had not been there before. There was just woods, as far as she could see—bare tree trunks and a carpet of brown leaves covering the forest floor.

Then she saw the deer. Its coat was so nearly the color of the brown leaves and the sunshine filtering through the trees, Ginnie thought at first she was imagining the shape of a deer. It was poised, head up, looking straight at her. For an instant they stared into each other's eyes.

Then a branch cracked somewhere. The deer turned and bounded off. As quickly as he had appeared, there was no sight or sound of him.

There were voices now. Geneva and her father were coming back. Ginnie waited till they were down from the rocks. Then she ran to meet them, softly, so as not to frighten the deer if he was hiding close by.

"I saw a deer!" she whispered. "I think he was a baby deer. He wasn't afraid of me at all!"

"Oh, I wish I had!" Geneva was dismayed.

"He's probably near us now," Mr. Porter said. "The brook's right over there. He may have come down for a drink."

Ginnie went along, trying to keep her feet from crunching in the leaves, and looking carefully around her. The wonder of seeing the deer glowed warmly inside her.

About midday they came upon a wider path. "See!" Mr. Porter pointed at a mark cut in a tree. "We're on the Appalachian Trail. This goes from Maine to Georgia. You could hike all that way if you wanted to."

They were on top of the world. On both sides of the ridge the rocks fell away to woods, and the woods rose into hills and valleys and farther hills. Maine to Georgia! A thrill rippled up Ginnie's spine.

They built another fire to cook their hot dogs. This time Ginnie helped. She wanted to know how to build a fire—how to do everything—if she was going to be a hiker!

As the smoke began to rise, Ginnie stood still suddenly, sniffing deeply. "Oh, what is it?" she cried.

"It's cedar," Mr. Porter told her. "Smells good, doesn't it?"

The sweet, pungent fragrance of the red wood was heavenly. Ginnie took deep breaths.

91

She wished they could stay here on top of the world, by the cedar fire, forever. She tucked a piece of cedar in her pocket to put in her bureau drawer.

"Well," Mr. Porter said, as they packed up, "do you think you like hiking for a hobby?"

"Yes!" Geneva shouted.

"Oh, yes!" Ginnie echoed.

"You were the girl," Mr. Porter said, "who was afraid of snakes or something in the woods."

"Oh, I'm not scared any more!" Ginnie told him earnestly. "I didn't know it was like this. I didn't know there were deer. Oh, I love it!"

Going back was shorter. Too short. When Ginnie got a glimpse of the road ahead, she stood still for a minute behind the others. She wanted to wrap the beauty and deep quiet around her. She pictured the deer, coming daintily down to drink, the woods carpeted with spring flowers, the pines weighed down with snow.

I'm coming back here, she thought, as she ran after the others. I'm coming every single time I can!

GENEVA TEASES TOO MUCH

Ginnie was deep in a book at the public library. She was reading about ferns and mosses, and the whispering of the other children around the book shelves was to Ginnie the sound of wind in the bare branches. Books about birds and wild flowers and trees were sprawled in a heap on the low table before her.

Ginnie read the last page, studied the last colored picture and closed the book. She looked up with a sigh and stretched slightly. She'd been reading a long time.

The lights were on in the library. Already the short November afternoon was drawing toward dusk. She'd better go. Ginnie picked out one of the books in the pile on the table to take home.

"Well!" Miss Appleton, the librarian, stamped Ginnie's card and slipped it in the front of the book. "I see you're reading nature books now instead of stories."

Ginnie nodded eagerly. "Yes," she explained, "because we all have to have hobbies for the hobby show at school. And Geneva and I have hiking and wild flowers and everything for ours."

"Isn't that nice!" Miss Appleton looked interested.

"I'm going to learn all about ferns and moss first," Ginnie went on. "And in the spring I'm going to learn all the wild flowers. And after that, I'm going to learn about trees and rocks and everything."

"That's quite a program." Miss Appleton handed her the book with a smile and turned to stamp the next child's card.

Miss Appleton is really nice, Ginnie thought, going down the library steps with her book. She'd never said anything to Miss

Appleton before. But it was easy to talk, now that she had something exciting to talk about.

Ginnie walked slowly along the street, her thoughts on the woods and all the things she was going to know about them. Maybe they'd have another hike soon. When spring came, they were going for a hike practically every Saturday.

Ginnie came out of her thoughts and looked around in surprise. Where was she? Absent-mindedly, she had taken the turn toward Red Robin Lane instead of Geneva's house.

A wave of homesickness swept over Ginnie. If only she could close her eyes and walk down Red Robin Lane, and then open them and see lights in her house. Lights, and Mother at the window! She wanted to tell Mother about her new hobby. The old lump swelled in Ginnie's throat. Without any guiding, her feet carried her slowly down Red Robin Lane.

Suddenly Ginnie jumped hastily to one side, nearly dropping her book. There was a scuffle of feet on gravel. Peter Ladd, coming down his driveway on his bike, jumped off and stopped it in time to avoid a collision.

They stood face to face. "Hello," Peter said in surprise.

"Hello." Ginnie's heart began fluttering nervously.

"Gee," Peter said. "Almost ran into you."

"I know." Ginnie couldn't think what else to say.

"Did you come home to stay?"

She shook her head.

"Oh," They were both silent. Then Peter said, "Have you still got that black cat that used to sit on your porch?"

Ginnie nodded. "Have you still got your dog?"

"Oh, sure."

What else could she say? Ginnie looked down and marked on the ground with her toe. Peter walked his bike a little way. Then he leaned it against the hedge and began to fix something.

"You got a hobby?" he inquired.

Ginnie looked up quickly. "Oh, yes!" she said. "Geneva and I have hiking for a hobby, and we're going to collect plants and wild flowers and everything."

Suddenly she wanted to tell Peter about hiking, just as she had wanted to tell Miss Appleton. "We went on a hike and cooked our *breakfast* outdoors!" she exclaimed.

"Did you?" Peter looked interested. "I often go on Scout hikes. We even stay all night sometimes."

Ginnie looked at him with amazed delight. Why, Peter must know what it was like in the woods early in the morning! "Don't you love it?" she cried.

He nodded. "Yeah, it's swell."

"Is that your hobby?" Ginnie inquired.

Peter shook his head. "No. Stamps. I've got a stamp collection."

"Oh," Ginnie said, "I remember."

"Say—" Peter had an idea. "Do you want to come and see my stamps?"

Ginnie was so surprised she could only stare for a moment. "Oh, n-not now!" she said hastily, stuttering in her confusion. "I have to go home."

"Oh." Peter sounded disappointed. "Well, you can come some other time if you want to."

97

"You mean—Geneva and me?" Ginnie asked.

Peter hesitated. He looked down and kicked the tire of his bike. "Do you have to bring her?" he asked finally.

Why, what did he mean—did she have to bring Geneva? Thoughts began tumbling through Ginnie's head. Didn't Peter want Geneva to come? Could that mean—could it possibly mean—he didn't like Geneva? Ginnie was stunned!

Suddenly she heard herself say a remarkable thing. "I guess I don't have to bring her," she said. "I can come tomorrow."

"O.K." Peter sounded relieved and pleased.

" 'By." Now Ginnie wanted to get away quickly. She felt shocked by what she had discovered. Peter didn't like Geneva! Why, everyone liked Geneva. Geneva was friendly, and she was lots of fun. Many times Ginnie had wished with all her heart that she had Geneva's quick tongue and ready laugh. She admired Geneva more than anyone she knew.

Of course Geneva did tease people. She teased Peter and copied him. Suddenly Ginnie remembered that time when Geneva tipped up Peter's seat and he sat on the floor! But everyone thought Geneva was funny when she did things like that.

Did they? A doubt crossed Ginnie's mind as she walked along in the dusk. *She* hadn't thought it was funny when Geneva teased her! Anyway, Peter didn't like Geneva. Ginnie still found it hard to believe.

That night she said nothing about meeting Peter. It did occur to her during school next day that she'd have trouble explaining. She hated to hurt Geneva's feelings.

After school Peter said, "See you at my house," and went off on his bike.

Maybe she could slip away. But no—Geneva was right there.

"Please tell your mother I'll be home pretty soon," Ginnie said, walking down the school walk backward.

"Where you going?" Geneva demanded.

Ginnie suddenly decided not to tell her. "Somewhere," she said.

"If you don't tell me, I'll follow you!"

Ginnie began to feel mad. She could see

why Peter didn't like Geneva. "All right then, follow me!" She turned on her heel. Geneva didn't have to be that way!

Geneva marched behind her. She'll follow me right there, Ginnie thought. She turned around and stopped. "If you have to know," she said, "I'm going to Peter's."

Geneva looked properly surprised. "Peter's! What are you going there for?"

"He asked me to. To see his stamps."

"Well, I'm going too."

"No, Geneva," Ginnie said.

Geneva looked hurt. "O.K., if you don't want me."

"Oh, I do, Geneva." Ginnie's heart melted swiftly. "Only Peter . . ."

"Oh," Geneva cried. "Peter doesn't want me! Mr. Stuck-up Peter!"

Oh, dear, Ginnie thought. "He isn't stuck up, Geneva," she said, "only you tease him and I don't think he likes it."

"Stuck-up Peter!"

Ginnie gave up and walked along. Geneva followed.

"Stuck-up Peter, stuck-up Peter!"

Ginnie began to be furious.

Then, suddenly, she remembered something. "If she gets fresh," Mrs. Porter had said, "just call her Jennie!" It wasn't nice. But Ginnie was really mad at Geneva. She turned around.

"Hello, Jennie!" she said softly. "Jennie, Jennie, Jennie!"

Geneva slowed down. "You stop!" she said.

"Jennie, Jennie, Jennie," Ginnie repeated. She added as an afterthought, "And I'll tell Peter to call you Jennie, too!"

Geneva hesitated. Then she turned and walked away without looking back. Ginnie was so mad she didn't care what Geneva did. She was so mad she forgot she felt shy about going to Peter's. She marched straight to Red Robin Lane, mad every inch of the way.

They had a lovely afternoon, looking at the stamps and playing with Taffy, the cocker spaniel. Peter's mother gave them some doughnuts and cider.

Peter had a knapsack and a Scout knife, and even a sleeping bag. Ginnie was fascinated with all the things for hiking and camping.

101

"Maybe," she said, clasping her hands as she thought of it, "Geneva's daddy would take us camping next summer! You too." She looked at Peter and shook her head seriously. "Geneva isn't really mean, Peter. She's nice!"

Peter looked down. "Oh, I know. She's O.K."

No, Peter didn't like Geneva. It worried Ginnie. But, at the same time, a little glow of pleasure stole over her. She and Peter were friends!

Ginnie went home so happy she didn't even cross the street to avoid speaking to a boy in her class, when she saw him coming. She said, "Hi!" instead, as cheerily as Geneva would have said it. And she smiled—a broad smile.

Geneva was reading in the living room when Ginnie went in. She didn't look up. Some of the good feeling went out of Ginnie. All right, if Geneva wanted to be mad.

At dinner Mrs. Porter noticed Geneva's silence and Ginnie's coolness. "What's the matter with you two?" she asked.

Geneva put her fork down on the table and burst into tears.

"Why, darling!" her mother exclaimed.

"She was mean to me!" Geneva got up and threw herself on her mother's lap. "She called me J-Jennie! She wouldn't let me go to Peter's. And she said she was going to tell Peter to call me Jennie!"

Mr. Porter gave Ginnie a puzzled look.

"Then I'm sure," Mrs. Porter said, "Ginnie had a good reason."

"I didn't care if she went," Ginnie burst out. "I wanted her to! But Peter didn't want her and I *know* it's because she teases him. And she said she was going anyway, and I didn't know what to do. So I called her Jennie, the way you said to."

"Good!" Mr. Porter said softly.

"Oh." Mrs. Porter smoothed Geneva's hair. "Well, you see, dear, people don't like to be teased."

"But I just wanted to be f-funny!"

"I know you did. You didn't mean to hurt anyone's feelings. But teasing isn't funny to the ones you tease."

Geneva went back to her chair, sobbing heartbrokenly.

Suddenly Ginnie could stand it no longer. She ran around the table to Geneva and threw her arms around her. "Don't cry, Geneva, please don't!" she begged, her head against Geneva's. "I was mean to call you Jennie, too. Honest, I'm sorry."

Geneva began to quiet down.

"I'll never call you Jennie again!" Ginnie declared.

Then she looked up and caught Mrs. Porter's eye. "Unless," she added slowly, watching Mrs. Porter's face, "you tease too much." Mrs. Porter gave a slight nod. Mr. Porter looked pleased.

Geneva drew a long, trembling sigh. "I won't tease Peter any more," she said. Then her eyes filled again. "But now Peter'll call me Jennie! And he'll tell all the kids and they'll call me Jennie!"

"No," Ginnie said. "He won't, Geneva. Because I didn't tell him."

THE POND IS FROZEN

The first week in December the weather turned unusually cold. "Oh, boy, ice skating!" Geneva said one morning as they headed into the icy wind on their way to school. "I bet the pond will freeze!"

Ginnie said nothing, but her heart sank. For the last two or three weeks all the kids had been talking about skating. All but Ginnie, who couldn't skate and hated the very mention of the subject. She was dreading the day when everyone would rush to the pond after school and she would be left out.

At dinner Geneva said, "I wish you'd skate, Ginnie!"

"I don't want to," Ginnie said quickly.

"But it's so much *fun!*"

"I'd rather read."

"Oh—stuffy!" Geneva was disgusted.

Ginnie went on eating in silence. The prospect was gloomy. She could pretend and pretend she didn't want to skate, but reading was going to be awfully dull when everyone else was on the pond. She hated being the only one who couldn't skate.

"If you'd like to, Ginnie," Mrs. Porter told her, "I'll go with you to buy some skates."

But Ginnie shook her head. "I don't want to." It was like roller skating. She was sure she never could. She'd just look silly.

Tuesday afternoon word went around. "The ice is hard!" 4-B couldn't get out fast enough. Geneva went tearing home to get her skates. Ginnie, looking for someone not in a hurry, fell in step beside Anna.

"Aren't you going skating?" Anna asked.

"Nope."

"Why not?"

"I don't want to."

"Gee," Anna said, "if I only had some skates, boy, I'd go!"

"Do you know how to skate?" Ginnie asked.

"No, but I bet I could learn."

Anna was looking pretty today. She was wearing a red and white checked dress that actually looked new.

"Come on home with me, Anna," Ginnie begged, "and do our homework. Geneva's mother will call the Matron for you."

Ginnie wanted to get indoors, where no one would see her and say, "What! Not skating?"

Anna loved to go to Geneva's house after school. Today Mrs. Porter gave the two girls each a jelly sandwich and poured glasses of milk.

"How nice you look, Anna!" she exclaimed. "Is that a new dress?"

Anna nodded happily. "Yes. And what do you think? After Ginnie and Geneva sent me that pretty sweater and skirt, the Matron said she guessed every girl needed a new dress sometimes, instead of all hand-me-downs. So the Committee Ladies are making them and one of them made this for me. Isn't it pretty!" Anna spun around for them to see all sides.

Ginnie and Mrs. Porter told her it was one of the prettiest dresses they'd ever seen. And so becoming!

Anna seemed restless today. As soon as they had finished their geography homework she threw down her book. "Let's go down to the pond and watch them skate," she said.

Ginnie went reluctantly. Everybody would ask why she wasn't skating. She tried to shrink inside her green wool hood, so no one would notice her. She shivered as they stood watching the bright, moving caps and scarves. The scrape of skates and the shouts and laughter of the skaters sounded clear and high.

"Oh, boy!" Anna said. Ginnie glanced at her. Anna's eyes were shining as she watched.

It must be fun, Ginnie thought, to glide so fast and so far, with the wind taking your breath. She gave herself a shake. She wouldn't admit, even to herself, that she'd like to skate. Of course, if she knew how . . . But she didn't. Everyone would laugh.

108

"Let's go, Anna," she begged. Her teeth chattered. Anna came along, her head turned to watch the skaters.

The next few days were a nightmare to Ginnie. Anna was her only companion after school. And in spirit even Anna was out on the pond. Never had Ginnie felt so completely alone.

On Friday the worst happened. Anna arrived in school radiant. Someone had given the Home children four pairs of skates. Anna had permission to skate that afternoon.

Ginnie was desperate. Now she had no one. All morning the dread of after-school aloneness hung about her like a fog.

By noon she had made up her mind. "I want to buy some skates," she announced at lunch.

"Goody!" Geneva clapped her hands.

"That's fine, Ginnie!" Mrs. Porter exclaimed. "I'll meet you after school with the car, and we'll go and get you some skates."

Half an hour after school, Mrs. Porter dropped Ginnie and her new skates at the pond. Geneva came up off the ice, balancing on her runners. "Hurry up, Ginnie, put them on," she cried. Geneva was rosy with wind and cold.

Ginnie sat down to put her skates on. How unprotected her hands felt when she took off her mittens. And her feet, without shoes. She slipped into the cold skate shoes, wondering why she had ever got into this.

Then she sat still and looked over the ice with fear rising inside her. She could see some girls holding Anna. Their laughter rang out when Anna went down in a heap.

"Come on, Ginnie," Geneva called impatiently.

Frightened out of her wits, Ginnie got slowly to her feet. The skates wobbled. "I can't walk!" she gasped.

"Yes, you can." Geneva held her arm tightly and they staggered to the edge of the ice, arms waving.

"Now try to slide," Geneva commanded.

Ginnie clutched Geneva with both hands. "Oh, Geneva!" she cried. "I can't! Don't leave me!" She was panic-stricken.

Lucy skated up to them. How could anyone stand up on that slippery ice?

"Come on," Lucy said, laughing. Together they tugged Ginnie out on the ice. Ginnie gripped them tightly, but her legs slid out helplessly from under her. She struggled and got her balance again. This went on for some time. Ginnie was in the middle of the pond by now. She didn't know how she had gotten there.

"You rest," Geneva said, "while we skate for a while." Off they sped, leaving Ginnie stranded. She stood rooted to the spot. She dared not move so much as a toe. Oh, if she ever got back on shore, she'd never try to skate again!

Looking around desperately for help, Ginnie's eyes lighted on Anna. Anna was stumbling and waving her arms. But she was moving. By herself. She was sliding her skates over the ice. Without thinking, Ginnie moved one foot. Down she went in a heap.

She looked around hastily. But no one was looking. Why, Ginnie thought in surprise, it doesn't hurt. And nobody pays any attention! Rising carefully on her hands, she managed to get to her feet.

When it was time to go home, Ginnie's ankles were so tired she couldn't hold them up. Geneva and Lucy, laughing, dragged her off the ice.

But once safely on the ground, loosening her skates, Ginnie was filled with excitement. I'm going to learn to skate! she thought. I can learn. I know I can. I almost did it once.

"Can we come back tonight?" she asked Geneva.

"Do you want to come again tonight?" Geneva laughed delightedly. "Maybe we can. Isn't skating fun? Aren't you glad you went skating?"

They rushed into the house. "Why, Ginnie," Mrs. Porter said, "I've never seen your cheeks so pink, dear, or your eyes so bright! My, but you look pretty!"

Geneva's father said he'd take them skating that night, since it was Friday. Ginnie could hardly wait to get back to the pond.

This time when she put on her skates her hands trembled with eagerness.

It was not as easy as she had thought it would be, though. She couldn't lift her feet. The skates shuffled over the ice. But again, when she took off her skates, she was sure that next time she would really glide off like a skater.

They were on the ice early Saturday morning. Ginnie shuffled and rested, shuffled and rested. She no longer cared how she looked. She had just one thought—to keep at it until she could skate.

Standing out on the ice, warm and panting, Ginnie watched a big boy glide round and round the pond. Suddenly she noticed how his feet kicked out behind. Timidly she tried lifting her own feet. That boy leaned forward, too. Ginnie bent over. And suddenly she was balancing—suddenly she was gliding forward on one skate, the other foot lifted.

I can skate, she thought. Not very well yet, but I'm really, really skating!

Sunday night the weather grew warmer.

There would be no more skating for a while— probably not till after Christmas, Mr. Porter said. Ginnie could hardly wait. When the ice was hard again, she would skate every minute she could. She'd be as good as Geneva and Lucy before long. She knew now that she could do it. Suddenly she thought, Why, if I can ice skate, I can roller skate too. I can do anything! I can be just like the others!

She was so happy Monday morning that she burst into a crowd of 4-B girls before the bell rang, to talk about skating. She was so happy she wrote a note and tossed it to Anna. Anna had not been on the pond that weekend. Ginnie had to tell her the wonderful news that she could almost, practically skate. And she was so happy she threw herself into the tag game at recess with a zest she'd never felt before. Her legs seemed to have new, livelier springs.

All of a sudden how easy it was to laugh out loud at nothing!

It was shortly after the skating that Miss Roberts sent Ginnie to the principal's office on an errand. Miss Yates thanked her for the message. Then the principal leaned back in her chair and looked at Ginnie thoughtfully.

"How are you getting along, Georgina?" she asked. "Are you enjoying school?"

"Oh, yes!" Ginnie's smile flashed out. Suddenly she remembered that first day, and how excited she had been but how scared. "I love school!" she exclaimed.

"You've made friends, haven't you?" Miss Yates asked.

"Oh, yes, lots of them!"

A warm, lovely feeling spread through Ginnie as she thought of 4-B and all her friends—Geneva and Peter and Anna, Lucy and Leonard.

"That's good," Miss Yates said, and smiled at her in a pleased way.

Ginnie skipped a little as she went down the hall. Climbing the stairs, she patted the cold round railing lightly.

"My nice school!" Ginnie said softly.

CHRISTMAS
VACATION

It was the last day of school before Christmas vacation. The Christmas play had been given. The 4-B room had been left behind, with its tinsel decorations and the warm, spicy scent of its Christmas tree for company.

Ginnie and Geneva and Anna walked home together. How strange and pleasant, going home at noon empty handed, without books.

The gray air was filled with excitement and the promise of more snow to cover the frozen gray on the ground. Wreaths had appeared on front doors, for tomorrow was Christmas Eve. Frosted store windows held piles of turkeys, celery tied with red ribbons, glossy red cranberries, and waxy oranges.

" 'God rest ye merry, gentlemen,' " Anna sang softly.

" 'Let nothing you dismay!' " Ginnie and Geneva chimed in. " 'For Christ our Lord and Savior was born on Christmas Day!' "

Ginnie gave a skip. Christmas! And that wasn't all. "I just can't wait!" she exclaimed.

Anna turned wondering eyes on her. "Are you really going to your grandmother's in an airplane?" she asked.

Ginnie nodded. "Yes! My daddy's coming to get me, and we'll be at Grandma's in time for supper tonight!"

She could hardly believe it herself. To see Mother and Daddy again after these long weeks! Mother couldn't leave Grandma yet, so Ginnie and Daddy were going there for Christmas.

"Please come over during vacation, Anna," Geneva said as they parted at the corner. Geneva was feeling mournful about Ginnie's going.

Ginnie looked up. She had been so busy

thinking about her own Christmas. "Are you going to have fun at the Home, Anna?" she asked.

"Oh, sure!" Anna said. "We have a tree, and the big ones help fill the little kids' stockings. And we have movies and candy and everything." She waved her hand. "Merry Christmas!"

"Merry Christmas, Anna!"

Still, as she and Geneva walked along, Ginnie wished Anna had a family of her own for Christmas.

"Shall I get dressed now?" she asked Mrs. Porter as soon as they finished lunch.

Mrs. Porter smiled at her. "You might as well. You're too excited to do anything else. Your things are on the bed."

"Oh, dear!" Geneva wailed. "I wish you didn't have to go!"

Ginnie looked back as she climbed the stairs. "I wish you could come too! But I'll be back in just a week. And I do want to see Mother and Daddy!"

She got into her plaid wool dress, brushed and braided her hair, and packed her brush and comb. There, on top of everything, were her Christmas presents for Mother and Daddy and Grandma—picture frames. She had made them in school. Each framed a picture of herself. Mother's picture showed her on ice skates. Mr. Porter had taken that one the Sunday she had almost skated. Daddy's snapshot was one taken on the hike. Grandma's was a picture of Ginnie holding Mumbo.

"You're going to miss some skating." Geneva was sitting on the foot of the bed, watching Ginnie get ready. Ginnie could tell Geneva was hoping, even now, that somehow or other she wouldn't go after all.

"Will there be some when I come back?" she asked anxiously.

"Of course there will be," Mrs. Porter assured her. "There'll be skating for a couple of months. Don't you worry, Ginnie."

Ginnie sighed happily. "In two months I can be a good skater, can't I?"

"And when you come back we have to begin planning the Valentine party we're going to give, too," Geneva said.

Ginnie suddenly dropped the handkerchiefs she was tucking in the pocket of her suitcase and ran to throw her arms around Geneva. Everything was wonderful! She was going to have Christmas with Mother and Daddy and Grandma. And after that she could look forward to skating and promotion and a new teacher. Already 4-B was talking about who that would be.

Then the Valentine party. And in the spring there'd be hikes and wild flowers and the hobby show. So many good times!

Geneva hugged her back.

"Just two hugging bugs," Mrs. Porter said, shaking her head at them as if it was hopeless. "What are you going to do when Ginnie goes home to her own house to live?"

Ginnie went back to her packing.

"Oh, but then she'll just be a few blocks away," Geneva explained, "and we can play every day."

"Well, anyway, I'll be back soon." Ginnie was looking in her bureau drawers to be sure she hadn't forgotten anything. "Don't forget to put my Christmas presents for everyone under the tree. They're in that drawer—one

120

for Mumbo, too." Presents from the Porters to Ginnie were already packed in her bag.

At last it was time to leave in the car for the airport. Daddy was coming in from Boston on one plane to meet Ginnie and take her on another plane to Grandma's.

The big airport with its loudspeakers, its roar of arriving and leaving planes, was a thrilling place. There was an extra bustle now, and the Christmas decorations gave an added excitement. Everybody, Ginnie was sure, was hurrying home for Christmas.

Ginnie clung to Mrs. Porter's hand until she saw Daddy in the crowd. Then she ran to meet him.

They were in their seats. Ginnie waved through the window to Geneva and Mrs. Porter. The door was shut now. The engines sputtered and roared into life. The plane was moving. It was speeding along the ground. Now the ground was falling away. They were rising. Off the ground! It was like a dream. Yet now that she was actually in the air, it seemed the most natural thing in the world to Ginnie to be flying.

121

She looked away from the window to the people in the plane. When she glanced back, the ground was far below. Ginnie looked down curiously. "Why, Daddy," she exclaimed, "the roads just go around in circles! They don't really go anywhere at all!"

Daddy looked too and smiled. "They're a fake, aren't they?" he said.

"See the ponds—like little looking glasses." Ginnie was fascinated by the strange earth below.

The color of the ground gradually changed from the gray of dirty snow to brown as they traveled. Where Grandma lived there was never much snow, never much cold weather. No skating there, Ginnie thought. She was glad she didn't live at Grandma's. Then darkness closed in, and millions of lights blossomed like stars below them.

Ginnie settled back. "Daddy," she said happily, "you know I can practically skate now!"

"So you wrote me," Daddy replied. "Well, that's certainly fine, isn't it! And what's this about hikes and hobbies?"

Ginnie laughed and told him all the things she had been doing.

They came down out of the sky at an airport much like the one they had left. Ginnie spied Mother in the waiting crowd and she broke away to run into her arms.

Then there was the ride home in Grandma's old car, with Mother driving. There was Grandma's big old house, smelling now of mince pie. There was Grandma, in her chair with a blanket over her knees, waiting for Ginnie with a welcoming smile on her face.

And finally there was bed, in the little room that had once been Mother's. Ginnie thought of Geneva. Then her eyes closed.

Saturday was busy and exciting. They had waited to buy the tree. "I thought you'd like to do that," Mother said. Ginnie and Daddy brought the tree home. They hung a wreath of pine and cones and red berries on the door, and Mother laid pine boughs over the fireplace.

Then Daddy brought the box of ornaments and lights from the attic. There was the little pink violin, the silver tip, and the heavy green ball that had been on Mother's first tree.

On Christmas Eve they sang carols, with Mother at the piano. Ginnie hung her stocking and went to bed to toss with excitement over what the morning would bring.

Christmas was fun, too. Ginnie had more presents than she had dreamed of—a wonderful doll and books and new clothes. And from Geneva a knapsack with a plate and cup and the other things a hiker needs for eating out of doors. Mrs. Porter's present to her was a wild flower guide.

It was a quiet day, with just the family there. Ginnie spent Christmas afternoon curled in a big chair, reading a new book.

But the week went slowly. The big house was so used to older people it seemed to Ginnie even the noises were heavy and solemn.

"I wish Geneva was here," she said to Mother. "Or I wish I could go skating or something."

On Tuesday a girl named Francie came to play. Francie's mother had been Mother's friend when she was little, and she seemed to be the only child Grandma knew. Mother left Ginnie and Francie in the living room and went to get them some ice cream and cookies.

Ginnie showed Francie her Christmas presents. "This is Dorothy, my doll," she said, presenting Dorothy to Francie. Francie took Dorothy in her lap. She fingered the blonde curls and the dress and pink shoes.

"And this is my knapsack," Ginnie announced proudly.

Francie just sat holding Dorothy, and stared blankly at the olive-green bag. Ginnie explained what it was for. "Have you got a hobby?" she asked.

Francie shook her head.

"I have," Ginnie said. "It's hiking. That's why I got the knapsack from my girl friend. And I got this wild flower guide, too." She turned the pages, waiting for Francie's exclamation at the pretty pictures. Francie just stared.

Ginnie closed the book. "Hiking's nice," she said, giving a small sigh. Oh, she could hardly wait to get back to Geneva! She cast about for something else to say to Francie. "Do you know how to ice skate?" she asked.

Another shake of the head.

"Oh, I forgot," Ginnie said. "There isn't any ice down here, is there? Skating's fun!"

At home, she thought, the kids were out on the ice this minute. She looked at Francie with distaste.

Mother tried to entertain Ginnie. They went to the movies and downtown for lunch. But there seemed so little to do.

"Dear Geneva," Ginnie wrote on Thursday, "I got a doll for Christmas. I have been to two movies. I can hardly wait to see you. Thank you for the knapsack and the wild flower book. I hope there will be lots of skating when I get back. I will see you soon. Loads of love from your friend, Ginnie."

Ginnie spent some time every day talking to Grandma. Grandma sat in her big chair in the front bay window, where she could see what went on outside and in. She loved to have Ginnie sit in the little low rocker and

126

tell her about school and all the things she and Geneva did.

"Seems to me," Grandma said, smiling at her, "you two have lots of fun!"

"Oh, we do!" Ginnie sighed happily. "Specially hikes—and ice skating." Her eyes were dreamy as she thought about it. "Everybody goes skating, you know, Grandma," she told her. "Even Anna."

"Now which one is Anna?" Grandma tried to think.

"Anna is the girl who lives in the Home," Ginnie explained. "She's a very nice girl and she's my best friend next to Geneva."

Grandma seemed interested. "Is Anna an orphan?"

Ginnie nodded. "Yes. And she used to never get a new dress. Only clothes the big girls outgrew. Anna didn't mind though— much," Ginnie added.

"Does she get new dresses now?"

"Oh, yes! She has a very pretty new dress a Committee Lady made. The Matron is good to Anna," Ginnie told Grandma earnestly. "And she lets her help take care of the littler children. Anna loves to take care of them!"

Grandma leaned her head against the back of her chair. "Anna sounds like a nice girl," Grandma said thoughtfully.

Ginnie was to leave on Sunday. Daddy, who had gone away again, was coming back for her. Ginnie didn't want to leave Mother. But the going-away ache stopped when she reminded herself of all the fun waiting.

It was Saturday night that Mother broke the news. She came and sat on the side of Ginnie's bed. Ginnie was in bed. "Darling," Mother said, "I have something to tell you."

Ginnie watched her expectantly. "What?"

"We thought," Mother went on, "that I could go home in a few weeks. But now the doctor says I ought not to leave Grandma. So I'm going to stay. And I don't want to be separated from my little girl any longer. So we decided you should go home and finish the term—that's only three weeks. Then you're coming back and have your spring term in the school here."

Ginnie stared at Mother. She didn't un-

128

derstand. "You mean . . . come here and live?" she said, puzzled. "At Grandma's?"

Mother nodded. "Just for a few months."

"But . . ." Now the meaning poured over Ginnie. Not go to Lincoln School? Not be promoted with her class? Ginnie's chin began to tremble. "But I wanted to be a good skater," she said in a strange voice.

Suddenly the realization of everything she would miss came flooding in on her. The Valentine party she and Geneva were planning. The hikes. The hobby show. All the fun! Ginnie turned away from Mother, flung herself face down on the pillow, and burst into tears.

EVERYONE HAS A SECRET BUT GINNIE

The second week of January brought a sleet storm. Now, at four-thirty, dark had already fallen. But the Porter living room was cheery with firelight, and Ginnie, Geneva, and Anna had been doing their homework.

Outside, the storm rattled the windows and hurled flat, wet flakes to plaster the pane.

Geneva closed her book with a yawn and slipped from her chair to the floor in front of the fire. Ginnie and Anna followed. Lazily, Ginnie reached over to the market basket at one side of the hearth. In the basket, a mound of soft fur all warm from the fire, lay Mumbo and her first baby, sound asleep. Mumbo gave a sleepy chirp as Ginnie dragged her out on her lap.

Anna leaned over to rub the black cat under the chin. "Wasn't it nice of Mumbo," she said, "to have a baby just when the old cat and her kittens were all given away!"

"Oh, dear." Geneva heaved a deep sigh. "The mother cat and the kittens are gone. In a couple of weeks you'll be gone, Ginnie, and Mumbo and the kitten, too. I won't have anyone!"

Ginnie stroked Mumbo's silky fur. She didn't answer for a minute. She didn't want to talk about going away. "Yes," she said finally. "But nobody knows except you two— and your mother, Geneva. Don't tell anyone, please!"

"But they'll find out when you go!" Geneva sounded impatient.

"But I don't want them to know before." Ginnie couldn't help feeling that if she pretended she wasn't going—if she didn't tell a soul—maybe, somehow, she wouldn't have to go.

"I'll miss you so much," Anna said sadly.

"It won't be any fun going on hikes with just Daddy," Geneva said gloomily. "You'll have to come, Anna."

Ginnie looked from one to the other and blinked back the tears. "Oh, you'll both be having so much fun!" she said. It seemed to Ginnie that all she wanted in the world was to be allowed to go to Lincoln School with her class. If only she could do that, she'd never, never be unhappy in her life again.

Mrs. Porter came in with the corn popper and a can of popcorn. "You three sound so gloomy," she said, "maybe this will cheer you up. Ginnie isn't going to China, you know." She shook some corn in the popper and handed it to Geneva. "I'll get the dishes and the butter and salt," she added.

When she came back they were all watching the corn. The hard kernels were bursting into blossom with soft, quick plops. The white popcorn flowers were packing the cage fuller and fuller. Mrs. Porter tipped the popperful into a yellow bowl.

"I won't have anybody to pop corn with or anything," Ginnie said with a sniffle.

"Now look, children," Mrs. Porter said cheerfully, "you've got to be sensible about this. You're not going away forever, Ginnie. You'll almost surely be home by summer. And you'll find girls to play with where your Grandma lives."

"No," Ginnie said, remembering Francie, "they're different. They aren't like the girls here. They don't know about hobbies. And there won't be any skating!" The tremble came into her voice again.

They all sat gloomily silent. Mrs. Porter passed soup plates full of buttery, salty popcorn. Wild gusts of wind-driven sleet pelted the panes.

"Did you tell Miss Roberts?" Mrs. Porter asked.

Ginnie looked up in alarm. "Oh, no! I don't want her to know!"

"But they'll have to know at school, dear. If you want me to, I'll tell her," Mrs. Porter said.

"O.K." Ginnie said with a sigh. "But ask her please not to tell anyone!"

"Oh, dear." Geneva groaned. Then she brightened. "I know!" she exclaimed. "Write your mother and tell her you don't want to go."

Ginnie thought that over, stuffing the crisp, buttery corn in her mouth. "No," she said slowly, "I can't. She'd feel bad." She sat staring into the fire. "I have to go."

They were all thoughtful. The only sounds were the slap of snow against the windows, the spit and crackle of the fire, the squeaky crunch of corn.

Then Mrs. Porter, Geneva, and Anna all started to speak at once.

"Hey!" Geneva said.

"I . . ." said her mother.

"Maybe . . ." Anna began.

They all stopped and looked at each other, each waiting for another to speak. Geneva started to speak again, then seemed to change her mind. "Oh, never mind," she said.

"I was just thinking," Mrs. Porter began.

"Well, you children eat your popcorn." She got up and went out to the kitchen.

Anna opened her mouth and closed it the second time.

"What were you going to say?" Ginnie asked.

"Nothing," Anna said. "I mean, I forget." She got to her feet. "Well, I better go. Thank you for the popcorn, Geneva."

Mrs. Porter looked in again. "If you'll wait a while, Anna, Mr. Porter will drive you home."

But Anna shook her head. "No, thanks, Mrs. Porter. I've got to do something before supper."

That night the family was sitting in front of the fire again when Geneva said, "Mother, come out in the kitchen a minute."

Ginnie glanced up absent-mindedly from her book as they went out. Once or twice she looked up, hearing long whisperings in the other room. But the book was interesting and she went back to it. Then she heard Geneva climb the stairs. Mrs. Porter came back to her chair.

Geneva was still upstairs at bedtime.

"Where's Geneva?" Ginnie asked, yawning.

"Oh, she had something or other to do," Mrs. Porter replied.

Geneva was standing between her bed and her desk when Ginnie went into the room. There was a guilty look about her.

"What are you doing?" Ginnie asked.

"Nothing!" But Geneva's eyes were dancing. Suddenly she spun around, holding her hands over her mouth. "Anyway, it's a secret! I can't tell you." And that was all Ginnie could find out.

Anna came home with them as usual the next day, but she was in a hurry. "I can't stay," she announced, "only I want to speak to your mother, Geneva."

"My mother? What do you want to speak to her for?" Geneva demanded.

"Oh, something." Anna glanced at Ginnie. "Only it's a secret. I can't tell."

Ginnie looked from one to the other. "You're the second one that's got a secret!" she exclaimed. But from the way Geneva and

Anna looked at each other, she didn't think it was the same secret. Geneva looked as mystified at Anna's secret as Ginnie felt herself.

Anna talked to Mrs. Porter for a while in the kitchen. When she came out she looked very important. "I'm sorry I can't stay. Goodby." And she was gone.

The snow that had started as a sleet storm turned into rain and slush, and the days that followed were as dark and gloomy as Ginnie's thoughts.

There was no skating these days. There'd be no skating until the rain and snow stopped and the pond froze again. Every day without skating was lost forever to Ginnie. I'll never learn to skate, she thought desperately.

One day Miss Roberts asked Ginnie to stay in a minute at recess. "Mrs. Porter told me about your leaving us, Georgina," she said. "I'm so sorry. "

Ginnie's eyes filled with tears.

Miss Roberts put an arm around her. "Don't be unhappy, dear," she said. "You'll be back next fall, in the same class."

Ginnie clamped her teeth together and

turned her head aside. "But I'll miss 4-A!" she said. "I'll miss—everything! And I won't— won't be here for the hobby show!" She threw her arms around Miss Roberts' neck to bury the sobs.

"There, there," the teacher said. Ginnie cried till the sobs subsided.

"You come into the teachers' room," Miss Roberts said, "and we'll wash away those tears with some good cold water."

Miss Roberts got her fixed up so there was hardly any puffiness around Ginnie's eyes when the children came in. Ginnie saw the teacher look thoughtfully at her several times during the day. As the pupils filed out at three-twenty, she drew Ginnie aside again.

"Georgina," she said, "don't worry. Some-times, you know, the things we worry most about never happen."

Ginnie looked at her teacher curiously. Why, Miss Roberts had a queer expression, almost as if she had a secret too.

Mrs. Porter sat at her desk writing when Ginnie and Geneva burst into the house that afternoon. She stood up quickly, holding a

letter in her hand. Her blue eyes were dancing.

"What are you doing?" Geneva demanded.

"And whose business is that?" her mother
retorted, wrinkling her nose at her. "I was
just writing a letter, if you must know. And
now I'm going to mail it." She walked into
the hall for her coat.

"I'll take it to the mailbox," Ginnie offered.

"No, thank you, dear, I need the exercise."
Mrs. Porter went out the front door.

Why, Mrs. Porter always gave her her letters to mail! Ginnie looked after Geneva's
mother, feeling a little puzzled. Did she imagine it? Or did Mrs. Porter have a mysterious
look? What was the matter with everyone?
Everyone had a secret but her.

THE SURPRISE

Ginnie stood in the center of Geneva's bedroom and looked around. Today she ought to pack. She knew that, but up till now she had refused to face it.

This was Saturday morning before the last week of the school term. Sometime next week she would leave for Grandma's, to be there when the spring term started.

Downstairs Geneva was practicing scales. *Do, re, mi, fa.* The front doorbell rang twice, loud and quick. The postman. Ginnie listened at the top of the stairs while Mrs. Por-

140

ter took in the mail. There might be a letter from Mother, telling when she must leave.

"Anything for me?" she called down.

"No, dear."

Ginnie went slowly back to the bedroom. Funny. She hadn't heard from Mother in over a week. Well, maybe she was busy taking care of Grandma. Maybe Daddy couldn't come for her next week.

Mrs. Porter looked in. "What's the matter?" she asked.

"I was going to begin packing my clothes," Ginnie said. "But I guess I won't, till I hear from Mother,"

"You just forget about it. I'll do your packing when it's time," Mrs. Porter told her. "Geneva's almost through practicing. You children run along out and go skating."

Ginnie fairly flew down the stairs. For a little longer she'd pretend she wasn't going away.

It was a beautiful day. The wind swooped over the ice, scooping up coldness. There had been skating now for nearly a week. Ginnie and Geneva had skated every day after school. Ginnie couldn't get enough skating. Each day she skated better and better.

The pond was crowded. Ginnie saw Lucy and Leonard and Peter and Marjorie. Even Anna was out this morning. Most of 4-B, Ginnie thought, as she sat down to put on her skates. She tied the laces tightly, stood up, and picked her way down to the ice. Geneva followed closely as Ginnie skated off.

Peter raced over the ice to meet them. "Hi!" Ginnie sang out, waving her hand.

"Hi!" Peter turned sidewise and stopped, breathless and beaming. "Isn't it swell? Hey," he said to Ginnie, "when's your . . ."

There was a shriek as Geneva, her arms waving wildly, grabbed at Peter and went down on the ice. Peter went down too. Ginnie skated off, laughing, before the two could untangle themselves and get on their feet.

The sun was dazzling this morning, the sky an intense blue. The wind stung Ginnie's eyes and cheeks as she headed for the far side of the pond, coasting easily on one skate, then the other. She could go on like this forever.

She turned as Peter caught up with her, and paused to catch her breath.

"What were you going to say?" she called out.

"Huh? Oh, I was just going to say when's— when are you going on a hike again?"

Ginnie was delighted. "Do you want to go?" she cried. Then she remembered. "Oh," she said. "I don't know when." She skated off. But the joy of the day was gone. She didn't know when she would ever hike again.

Of course Peter had no idea that she was going away. She had stuck to her resolve not to tell a single person.

When Ginnie skated back into the crowd again the 4-B children were clustered together.

"I wish Miss Roberts would be our teacher again next term," Marjorie was saying. "Sometimes teachers are promoted too."

"But Miss Butterworth is nice," Anna said.

"Miss Butterworth!" Geneva echoed. Her eyes began to dance. "Here's what Miss Butterworth looks like." She lifted her chin, pressed her lips together, and stretched her neck as high as it would go. Suddenly she caught Ginnie's eye. Geneva hastily dropped her pose. "I didn't mean to," she said quickly. "I like Miss Butterworth."

Anna turned then and saw Ginnie standing beside her. Her eyes lighted up. "Oh, Ginnie!" Anna said. "I'm so glad . . ."

Geneva suddenly let out a screech and grabbed Anna's hand. "Come on, Anna, skate with me!" she cried, almost pushing Anna over in her eagerness. She pulled Anna along.

Ginnie frowned, looking after them. What ailed Geneva, pushing everyone around? But at least she was better about teasing and copying people.

They went home for lunch and came right back. As the shouts and laughter from the pond floated to meet them Ginnie thought, "I'm not really going away. It's just a bad dream."

She couldn't believe that next Saturday, and the one after, all this would be going on here as usual, while she was far away in Grandma's silent house.

By four-thirty the sun had gone. The air

was gray and bleak and Ginnie's ankles were tired. Geneva was ready to leave, too. The crowd began to thin out.

"Hey," Peter said, as they all tugged on their shoes with cold fingers, "come on over and see the new stamps I got. They're swell."

"Oh . . ." Ginnie wanted to go home and thaw out before the fire. She felt cold and a little gloomy. But Geneva and Anna seemed eager to see the stamps.

"Yes, let's!" Geneva agreed.

"I can stop a minute," Anna added.

Well, O.K., Ginnie thought. She slung her skates over her shoulder and trailed along with Anna. Peter and Geneva were ahead, talking busily. They were quite good friends, now that Geneva had stopped her teasing.

It was dusk. Cold blue shadows lay across the snow and lamps were being lighted in the houses. The winter twilight made Ginnie homesick.

But what was she homesick for? For Mother? Geneva's house? Her own home? Ginnie felt forlorn and confused. All the happy days seemed to be over. A lump rose in her

145

throat and a tear rolled down, wet and hot against her cold cheek.

Anna seemed in a hurry, but Ginnie's feet dragged.

Ahead of them, Peter and Geneva had stopped in front of Peter's house, and Geneva was shouting something back to Anna and Ginnie.

"What?" Ginnie asked, as she and Anna came up.

"Look!" Geneva sounded excited. She was pointing at something beyond.

What was she talking about, anyway? Ginnie's eyes followed the pointing arm uncertainly. Then, slowly, they focused where Geneva was pointing. Ginnie stood still and stared, not understanding. She couldn't believe what her eyes told her.

Her own house, next door to Peter's, was lighted from top to bottom.

"Why . . ." Ginnie felt dazed.

"Maybe it's burglars!" Peter said cheerfully.

"Silly!" Geneva scoffed. "Burglars wouldn't turn on all the lights! "

146

"Let's go see," Anna suggested.

But Ginnie waited no longer. Suddenly she was running. She was running away from the others, on down the sidewalk. She was running up the path to 82 Red Robin Lane. Ginnie's knees were shaking.

She pushed open the door, and ran straight into Mother's arms as Mother came in from the kitchen!

It was several seconds later that, laughing or crying—she hardly knew which—Ginnie pulled back to look into Mother's face. "Are you going to stay?" she asked breathlessly.

Mother nodded. "Yes."

But Ginnie had to be sure. "Then I can still go to Lincoln School, can't I, and be promoted?"

"Indeed you can."

"And—and I can go skating, and on hikes to collect flowers for the hobby show?"

"Yes, dear."

Ginnie gave a deep sigh.

She had been dimly conscious of hearing someone in the cellar. Now there were footsteps on the cellar stairs. The door opened and Daddy came up, carrying a load of firewood. Ginnie threw herself against him, hugging logs and all.

"And look who else is here!" Mother said.

Grandma was coming slowly downstairs.

Geneva and Anna were there now, and in the background Ginnie was conscious of Peter, a broad grin on his face. Everyone was talking and laughing.

"But what happened?" Ginnie kept asking Mother. "Why did you come home? I thought . . . I thought . . ."

"Well, you see," Mother explained at last, when she could make herself heard, "when we saw how you hated to leave, and how much all your friends wanted you to stay, we didn't know what to do. The doctor said Grandma mustn't be left alone. But," Mother went on, "it was really the letters that decided us."

"What letters?" Ginnie demanded.

"Why, the letters from Geneva and Anna."

Ginnie looked in bewilderment at her two friends. Each wore a guilty expression. "And

148

the letter from Mrs. Porter, and then Miss Roberts," Mother added.

Anna and Geneva were looking at each other queerly. "Did you write a letter?" Geneva demanded.

Anna nodded. "Yes, but I didn't know you did."

"And I didn't know my mother did, either!" Geneva exclaimed. "She never told me."

Ginnie still felt confused.

"Don't you remember, Ginnie," Geneva said, "that day it snowed, you said you couldn't ask your mother to let you stay because it would make her feel bad? So I thought I'd write and tell her I wished you could stay . . ."

"So did I! I got the address from Mrs. Porter," Anna broke in.

"I remember," Ginnie said slowly. So that was the secret they all had! Even Miss Roberts.

"Well, the letters worked," Daddy said.

"Yes," Mother added. "Grandma said she'd never get well if she took you away from everything. So all in a hurry we closed the house—and here we are!"

Ginnie suddenly looked at Geneva. "Geneva Porter, did you know they were coming?"

Geneva nodded, giggling.

"It was Geneva's idea to make it a surprise," Mother said. "I phoned, day before yesterday, but you girls weren't home . . ."

Geneva interrupted. "You were out skating, Ginnie, and I got home from my music lesson. And Mother told me and I thought it would be fun to keep it a surprise. So I made her promise not to tell you."

Ginnie looked at Anna and Peter. "Did you know?"

They nodded, grinning.

"I told them," Geneva said. "Only they almost forgot and told when we were skating. I had to nearly knock them down so they wouldn't. And we brought you over here on purpose, Ginnie. It wasn't really to see Peter's stamps at all!"

Ginnie took a deep breath and looked at Mother. She could hardly believe it. "Oh," she remembered, "my clothes. They're all at Geneva's."

150

"No," Mother said. "They're upstairs. Mrs. Porter brought them this afternoon, along with a pan of baked beans. I smell those beans now!" Mother hurried to the kitchen.

"Well," Geneva turned away reluctantly, "I guess we have to go."

Ginnie and Daddy went with them to the door. "Good-by. But I'll see you at the pond tomorrow. And Monday at school. Oh, Geneva!" Ginnie cried suddenly. The three girls hugged each other, laughing and laughing.

Ginnie closed the door after them.

"Well," Daddy asked her, "glad to be home?"

She nodded happily and they went into the kitchen, their arms around each other. Ginnie paused suddenly. Under the gas range stood Mumbo's basket. She stooped and pulled it out. There was Mumbo, giving her baby such an extra special bath that every lick of her rough pink tongue sent the kitten sprawling. But he liked it. His tiny rattling purr was a sound of pure contentment. Gently Ginnie pushed the basket back under the stove.

She remembered something else. "Oh," she

151

cried, "I'll be here for the Valentine party, won't I! Only I was going to help give it."

Mother was taking the pan of fragrant, bubbling beans from the oven. "Maybe Geneva wouldn't mind if you had the party here," she said.

"Could I?" Ginnie clasped her hands and spun round and round the kitchen.

At supper they talked about the plans for Grandma.

"I'm better already," Grandma declared. "I stayed too long in that lonely old house."

"We're going to find Grandma a bungalow close by," Daddy explained, "and a woman to do the work."

"And I've been thinking about what you told me"—Grandma sipped her tea thoughtfully—"about your little Anna friend. Do you think she'd like to come and live with me?"

Ginnie put down her fork in astonishment.

"Mrs. Porter tells us," Mother said, "that Anna is a fine child, intelligent and sweet as she can be. Of course she's only ten . . ."

But she's smart," Grandma put in. "You could tell that from her letter."

"We thought Grandma and Anna could sort of take care of each other," Mother said. "Grandma needs someone, so she won't be all alone nights."

Ginnie got her breath. "Oh, Grandma!" she gasped. "Oh, Anna would just love to have a real home! Oh!" She couldn't sit still. She got out of her chair to jump up and down. "And she'd take care of you, Grandma," she added earnestly. "She takes care of the little children in the Home."

"It's time somebody took care of her," Grandma said.

"Could she call you Grandma?" Ginnie asked.

"Of course."

"Then she'd be a cousin, sort of," Ginnie said. "I'll really have a cousin."

She gazed into space in a happy dream. "Please may I be excused?" she asked.

She ran into the kitchen and gathered Mumbo and the black kitten in her arms. Carrying them both, her cheek against the soft fur, she went slowly back to the dining room. In the doorway Ginnie paused.

153

Was all this a dream? Candlelight gleamed on the blue and white dishes. The soft glow gave a shine to Mother's brown eyes, lighted Grandma's white hair and Daddy's face as he turned to smile.

No, this was real.

I'll always remember this minute, Ginnie thought. I've never, never been so happy before!